DAUGHTERS OF THE MOON

moon demon

Also in the
DAUGHTERS OF THE MOON
series:

DAUGHTERS OF THE MOON

moon demon

LYNNE EWING

VOLO

HYPERION/NEW YORK

First Edition
5 7 9 10 8 6
Printed in the United States of America

Library of Congress Cataloging-in-Publication Data
Ewing, Lynne.
Moon demon/Lynne Ewing.— 1st ed.
p.   cm. — (Daughters of the moon ; 7)
Summary: As her sixteenth birthday approaches, Vanessa, a girl with the power to
become invisible, worries that the other goddesses are shutting her out, fears a demon
sent by the Atrox, and desires a handsome stranger.
ISBN 0-7868-0849-7 (hc)
[1. Supernatural—Fiction. 2. Los Angeles (Calif.)—Fiction.] I. Title.

PZ7.E965 Mo 2002
[Fic]—dc21   2001051828

Visit www.volobooks.com

*For Donna Peters and her language arts
students at Elida Middle School in Elida, Ohio,
with special thanks to Kyle Dickrede and
Matt Inkrott*

During the Peloponnesian War a brave Athenian soldier fell desperately in love with the daughter of his commander. He asked for her hand in marriage but she had to refuse. Having dedicated her life to the goddess Selene, she had vowed not to marry until an evil power called the Atrox was vanquished. The soldier swore to destroy the dark force and free his beloved from her vow.

He traveled day and night until he came to the western side of the river Oceanus. There he passed through groves of barren willows and poplars until he found the cave that led to Tartarus, the land of the dead. He entered it, and when he reached the impenetrable darkness, demons swarmed around him.

A towering black cloud surged toward him. He

knew it was the Atrox. But instead of trembling with fear, he became intoxicated with his own bravery; he alone had the courage to face the Atrox. If he destroyed it, he would not only win his bride, but also become as powerful as any of the immortal gods.

Pride overtook him as he shot his arrow. A terrible scream pierced the misty air. Then the unimaginable happened. The Atrox surrendered to him and humbly offered a gift of gold ankle bands in tribute.

The young man, eager to return to his love and flaunt his victory, clasped the heavy metal bands around his legs, but as he did, flames ravaged his body and the evil he had set out to destroy consumed him. The Atrox had tricked him and given him not ornaments but shackles, condemning him to an eternity of servitude. Demons carried him away from the underworld and cast him out from Earth.

Over the centuries many people have seen the young soldier in the night sky and thought him only a falling star. He wanders the universe alone, unable to return to Earth unless summoned by his master, the Atrox.

CHAPTER ONE

V ANESSA AWOKE WITH a start, whispers rustling in her ears. She listened, but the only voices she heard came from the sports announcers on the late-night rerun of the Lakers game. She had fallen asleep on the couch again, dressed in a worn T-shirt and red boxer shorts, waiting for her mother to come home.

She sat up and swung her bare feet onto the shaggy rug. Someone had been nudging her awake. The touch couldn't have been from a dream. It had felt too real; fingers caressing her forehead, neck, and shoulder before resting on her thigh.

"Mom?" she called, wondering if her mother had been trying to wake her and finally given up. When no one answered, her heart began to pound. Could an intruder be in the house with her?

Her eyes darted around the living room, searching for something that didn't belong. Changing lights from the TV twitched against the wall and made the chairs, lamps, and coffee table shimmer, but she didn't see anything that might betray a prowler. Maybe being alone at night again while her mother worked had made her imagine things.

She picked up the remote, aimed at the TV, and pressed the OFF button. The house fell silent as shadows spread out to the corners.

A draft made her turn. She rubbed her arms against the sudden chill. The beige drapes ballooned, then fell back, only to swell out again with a cold breeze. Earlier she had opened the side window, but she thought she had closed it before settling down to watch TV with her buttered popcorn and root beer.

She slipped from the couch and crossed the room, then stopped in front of the drapes and pulled back the velvet fabric until she had enough space to peer out without being seen from the street.

Papers and leaves tumbled across the lawn and gathered against fences and parked cars. The Santa Ana winds were stirring, and everyone knew those devil winds wreaked havoc on the minds of Angelenos. She probably *had* left the window open. It wouldn't be the first time. Maybe in a dream she had confused the wind's wailing for someone whispering to her. And the breeze might have given her sleepy mind the impression of hands nudging her awake.

She started to close the window, but stopped when she saw round fingerprints on the glass. Her breath caught. The smudges were too large to belong to her. Could her mother have come home without waking her and opened the windows before going on to bed? That didn't make sense. An open window without a screen was an invitation to thieves. Her mother knew that.

Vanessa glanced at the red digital readout on the cable box. Three o'clock? Her mother had said she'd be home before two. The director always called a wrap by midnight when he did exterior night shots in south-central L.A. She hurried to the stairs and started up to her mother's bedroom when something as soft as a kiss brushed against her neck. She jerked back, cringing, then whipped around and looked frantically both ways, but saw nothing.

Her hands clasped the banister. She ignored the fear creeping over her and examined the living room. The muscles in her back tightened as her body tensed, ready to fight. Could someone be crouched behind the sofa, watching her? Or hidden in the closet only a few feet away? She ran her trembling fingers around the nape of her neck. Maybe it had only been a strand of hair falling from her ponytail. She scooped up the loose tangles and redid her tiger-print scrunchie, then paused and listened. She wasn't afraid of a prowler, not the human kind, anyway. But she had other enemies in the night. They had been trying to destroy her since she had discovered who she was.

"*Tu es dea, filia lunae,*" she whispered, repeating the words Maggie had spoken to her when they first met. Even now the words soothed her and filled her with awe.

She had always known she was different from other people because she had a unique ability that she kept hidden. Even her mother didn't know. As she grew older, she had assumed her power was the result of some genetic defect or exposure to radiation. It wasn't until she met her best friend, Catty, that she found someone else who was like her. But she had never imagined the truth. Even now it was hard for her to believe. She was a goddess, a Daughter of the Moon, and she was here to protect people from the Followers of an ancient evil called the Atrox.

She considered this now. Most Followers were Initiates—kids who had turned to the Atrox and wanted to prove themselves worthy of join- ing its congregation. Maybe a gang of them had stolen into the house and were playing a cat-and-mouse game with her. She had nothing to fear from them. But there were other powerful Followers who could turn to shadow and skate through the night unseen. Maybe one of them was hiding stone still in the dark, waiting for a chance to attack.

She glanced at the amulet hanging around her neck and studied the face of the moon etched in its metal. It had been given to her at birth, and she never took it off. It glowed when Followers were nearby. Right now it looked like an ordinary charm; if someone were in the house with her, it had to be a human prowler. The muscles in her back began to relax. Maybe she should play a little game of her own. Why not? It would teach the intruder not to go scaring people in the night. She smiled as she imagined the shocked look on the intruder's face when she became a misty form and flowed through his arms. That was her gift. She could become invisible.

Quiet footsteps crept across the upstairs hallway.

"Wrong house," she whispered. She would cure this one of his need to steal.

She relaxed her mind and let her body dissolve. Bone and tendon quivered until her arms, hands, and fingers looked like black specks waving in the dark. Soon she was free from gravity and drifting up the stairs.

But as she twisted through the gloom, something foreign tangled with her invisible body. It wove through her with a furry tickle, leaving a pungent scent of decay. It didn't have the sensation of steam, dust, or smog. She curled back, trying to escape the sickening smell, but whatever it was moved with her, sinuous like a snake, coiling around her. She twirled, then sprang forward, but it held her. The air became thick and gluey, her cells no longer able to pull in oxygen through osmosis.

She concentrated, gathering all her energy, then sped forward and pierced the gummy barrier. Her skin tingled as she materialized on the edge of the third step. She teetered, arms swinging for balance, then fell and hit the floor with a loud thump. Pain spun around her head, but worse was the sickening taste of decay in her mouth. She sat up and spit, then took long, gasping breaths like a swimmer who had stayed under water too long.

When her heart slowed and her breathing came in even draws, she leaned against the wall next to the first step and rubbed at the soreness in her elbow. She studied the stairwell. She wondered if viruses ever floated in a mass. It seemed possible, or maybe, like Santa Monica Bay, Los Angeles was becoming polluted by bacteria.

"Great," she muttered, imagining the flu she'd have in a couple of days.

She started to stand when a floorboard snapped in the corner. She crouched low, peering through the posts supporting the banister. She saw nothing, but could not erase the feeling that someone was in the room with her.

Another creak, then one more pop of wood as if a person were taking slow, easy steps toward her. Only immortal Followers had the ability to become invisible. She glanced again at her amulet, but it lay cold and still against her chest. It couldn't be a Follower, not any kind she knew about anyway.

She stood slowly, her heartbeat thudding, and tried to quiet her thoughts. Her mind sensed danger; something bad was in the room.

"O Mater Luna, Regina nocis, adiuvo me nunc." The words came unsolicited from her lips, and she gasped. That prayer was only said in times of grave peril.

Even if it was her imagination, she wasn't going to wait to find out. She eased toward the door, watching for a tremor of black that would reveal a Follower hidden in the gloom.

When she was at the door, she slid her hand behind her and felt across the wood until she found the smooth brass knob. She wrapped her fingers tight around it, her eyes still probing the dark.

Then instinct took over. She spun around, fumbled for the dead bolt, found it, jerked it back, and turned the knob. Wind rushed into the house and yanked the door from her hand, smacking it against the wall with a loud rap. The impact made a picture fall. Glass shattered and skidded across the floor.

She started to walk outside, but the feeling of someone close behind her made her leap from the porch. She sensed someone calling her, but she didn't want to turn around and see who it was. She sprinted down the sidewalk, red and fuchsia petals from the bougainvillea swirling into her face, the bottoms of her feet slapping the gritty concrete.

When she reached the olive tree, someone darted from the garage and grabbed her shoulder.

Vanessa jerked away, lost her balance and tumbled to the ground.

CHAPTER TWO

VANESSA TRIED TO CONTROL her fall. She skidded, scraping skin on her hands and knees. Ignoring the pain, she sprang up, and ran, arms pumping hard at her sides. Wind rumbled through the branches overhead, spilling a torrent of leaves over her.

She became aware of footsteps, pounding the sidewalk behind her, and ran faster.

"Vanessa, it's me!" her mother yelled.

Vanessa slowed, glanced over her shoulder, and stopped.

"What's wrong?" Her mother's brown hair

whipped around her head, and in the amber light from the street lamp, her face looked anxious.

Vanessa hurried back to her. "Someone's inside."

Her mother's eyes widened, and she pulled Vanessa close as if to protect her. "Are you all right? You're not hurt?"

Vanessa shook her head and stared at the doorway. Jagged shadows from the palm fronds danced across the porch, making it appear as if someone were moving in the entrance of the small house.

"You saw someone?" her mother asked. Her free hand rummaged into her large shoulder bag and pulled out a purple cell phone. She flipped it open as a sudden gust shrieked around them.

"No, not exactly," Vanessa confessed after the wind died.

"You heard something, then." Her mother punched in 911 and held her thumb over the send button.

"I fell asleep on the couch again. I think someone woke me," Vanessa explained, but now everything that had happened felt more like pieces of a dream. Could she have imagined it all?

Her mother relaxed. Her grip loosened and she managed a slight smile. "Are you sure you weren't dreaming?" She started walking toward the house.

"I heard footsteps and saw fingerprints on the window." Vanessa pointed to one of the small windows on either side of the larger one.

Her mother stopped and studied the open window. "Show me," she said and took a determined step forward, her chunky shoes beating a fast clip.

Inside Vanessa flicked the wall switch near the door. The lamps cast a gentle glow over the green couch, ocean-blue rugs, and hardwood floor. The light scattered any remaining doubt. Whatever had been there before, if anything, was gone now. The room gave her the same feeling of security that it always had.

Her mother drew back the drapes and studied the windowpane. "I don't see anything."

The fingerprints that had been there earlier were gone.

"Let's check upstairs anyway," her mother said, closing the window with a loud slam and locking it.

Twenty minutes later every light in the house was blazing, and they had found nothing. Vanessa took cotton balls and a bottle of peroxide to the living room and sat on the couch. Her skin stung as she cleaned the scrapes on her palms and knees. She appreciated that her mother had believed her, but right now she felt as if she had been cursed with an overactive and weird imagination.

"I'm sorry I was so late." Her mother set her cell phone down on the coffee table, then snapped her fingers as if she had remembered something. "Come outside with me. I hope we haven't missed it."

Vanessa followed her back outside to the middle of the street.

When they stepped out from under the umbrella of trees, her mother looked up and pointed. "There."

A frosty ring circled the full moon. The halo was breathtaking, muted red toward the inside and blue outside, but it felt like a bad omen to Vanessa. She started to shiver as an old memory came back to her.

Her mother turned to her. "I thought you'd love seeing the ring around the moon. That's why the director kept us so late. He was hoping it would go away so he'd be able to film. Then the wind started up. It blew down props, and when it started toppling the camera equipment, he sent us home."

Hot tears pressed into Vanessa's eyes. "Don't you remember, Mom?"

"Remember what?"

"The night Dad died, there was a ring around the moon." Vanessa had been only five then. Her father had worked as a stunt coordinator for the movies. She had seen him dive from speeding cars and tenth-floor windows. So she hadn't understood that the helicopter accident was real. That night she remembered creeping from her bed to see if her father's truck was home. And when she had looked out her window, she had seen a ring circling the full moon.

"There couldn't have been one, Vanessa." Her mother started walking back to the house, her steps slow now as if she were concentrating on her own memory. "I would have remembered something that unusual."

"The ring feels like . . . like it's a warning," Vanessa said. "Something bad is going to happen."

Her mother stopped and waited for Vanessa to catch up to her, then kissed the top of her head. "Don't go superstitious on me," she said softly. "Moon haloes are nothing but light passing through ice crystals in the clouds."

"Then why didn't the wind blow the clouds away?" Vanessa asked as another vigorous gust slapped around them.

Her mother stopped as if considering, then shrugged. "I'm not a weatherman. Come on."

They went back inside and her mother closed the door. "Vanessa," she started with a tone that made Vanessa dread what was coming next. "You've been acting a bit on edge. Is something wrong?"

"What do you mean?" Vanessa went to the kitchen, picked up the dustpan and broom and carried them back to the living room.

"Tonight you thought someone had broken into the house, and the other night I found you checking the locks on the windows downstairs after we had gone to bed."

"That's pretty normal in Los Angeles, Mom." Vanessa started to sweep up the broken glass.

Her mother folded her arms across her chest. "You've been so high-strung lately. That just isn't like you."

Vanessa stopped sweeping. "What's like me, Mom? Just tell me. What am I supposed to be like?"

Her mother paused as if Vanessa's sudden anger had caught her off guard. When she began again, her words were more careful. Vanessa sensed she was trying to avoid a fight.

"Are you upset about your birthday coming up? The closer it gets, the edgier you become, and

I don't understand why. Most girls look forward to their sixteenth birthday."

"It's not like I'm getting a car or anything," Vanessa mumbled and swept the glass into the dust pan.

"Vanessa, you know I'd get you one if I could afford it."

The hurt look on her mother's face made Vanessa feel guilty. She started to apologize, but something inside her wouldn't let her. Why was she the one who always had to do it? Instead she carried the dustpan and broom back to the kitchen.

"Is there something you're keeping from me?" Her mother paused and adjusted some sketches pinned to the bulletin board above her worktable, then she turned back, her voice nervous. "Is Michael putting too much pressure on you? Maybe now that you're getting older, you feel like you have to—"

"Mother!" Vanessa dropped the dustpan in the trash. The glass clinked and jingled to the bottom.

"All right." Her mother looked wounded, her forehead pinching into a frown. "I just want you to know that I'm here for you."

Vanessa retrieved the dustpan and hit it once against the inside of the trash can, then set it beside the refrigerator with the broom. Finally she looked at her mother, and for the first time noticed she was wearing a shimmering red skirt over yellow leggings and a large, bulky, canary-colored sweater. She dressed in ways that some-times embarrassed Vanessa, but that was her job. As a costume designer she wore clothes before anyone even knew they were in style. But not everything she concocted became a trend. No way was this one going to make the fashion magazines. Vanessa couldn't stop the grin creeping across her face.

Her mother misunderstood her smile. "I love you, too, baby." She spread her arms wide, then hugged Vanessa, rocking her back and forth.

Vanessa laughed, releasing her tension. She looked over her mother's shoulder at the kitchen calendar. Her birthday was less than a week away now. Each day had been crossed off with a red felt pen, counting down to the fourteenth. Her mother had done that for as long as Vanessa could remember.

Maybe she *was* upset about her birthday. After all, it meant she only had a year left to make the most important decision of her life. She didn't know yet if she'd have the courage to choose. What happened if she couldn't? Her gift only lasted until she was seventeen, and then there was a metamorphosis. It happened to all the Daughters.

Maggie had explained most of the mysteries of being a goddess to her, but no one really knew what happened to the ones who made the change. Maggie only knew that the ones who were too frightened to make the transition remained human but without their powers and with no memory of what they had once been.

"Talk to me, Vanessa." Her mother patted her back. "What's happened to us? You used to talk to me about everything."

Not everything, Vanessa thought, but maybe

she should tell her mother the truth. It wasn't as if other people didn't know. Catty's mother knew. So did Tianna's boyfriend, Derek. Jimena had told Serena's brother Collin, and since Collin was also Jimena's boyfriend, that meant Vanessa was the only one who didn't have someone to confide in. Maybe that's why she had been feeling so lonely.

She pulled back. "Mom, I'm going to tell you the truth." She took a deep breath, hoping that her mother's heart was strong. She started pacing. "You're not going to believe me, but I'm——"

A violent crash rocked the house. Vanessa gripped her mother's arm, and stood in front of her, as she scanned the kitchen looking for the enemy.

"Vanessa!" her mother protested, pushing around her. "It's the patio. The wind blew the roof off."

A gust rattled the sliding glass door as her mother walked over to it and switched on the back-porch light. Splintered pieces of redwood were scattered across the concrete slab. The pads from the lounge chairs had blown away and fallen crossbeams had shattered the glass table top.

"Thank goodness some of it's still standing," her mother said, as if she had been mentally calculating the cost of repairs.

The support beam and lintels were still in place.

"I'd better go outside and make sure nothing is caught on a utility line." She grabbed a flashlight and slid the door open.

Wind burst inside, knocking over the napkin holder and saltshaker. Paper napkins fluttered around the kitchen.

Vanessa spoke with sudden remorse, "Mom, I'm sorry. I don't mean to—"

"I know," her mother interrupted. "I was your age once, Vanessa. It's hard." She closed the sliding glass door and turned on the flashlight.

Moonlight bathed her mother as she stepped over the broken wood. She ducked under the hibiscus bush, then pointed the yellow flashlight beam at the low-pitched gabled roof, and drew it along the eaves, her red skirt lashing around her.

She waved once, then disappeared behind the side of the house.

Vanessa walked over to the calendar and tapped the wall. Her birthday was only one small part of her problem. She might be the most popular girl at school, but all at once it felt as if she'd paid too high a price for that honor. She didn't even know who she was anymore. She was letting too many people define her and she didn't want to spend her last year as a goddess being the person other people wanted her to be. She needed to do something drastic before she lost herself completely.

Then she thought of Michael Saratoga. He was the only person she felt really comfortable with. Maybe that's why she'd been toying with taking their relationship to another level. She hadn't discussed that with anyone, not even her best friend Catty. But she'd been considering asking Michael to . . .

"Vanessa."

She whipped around. She hadn't heard her mother come back inside.

"Your face is beet red." Her mother's cold palm pressed against her forehead. "Do you have a fever? You're coming down with something. You'd better get up to bed."

"Okay." Vanessa nodded, but her thoughts remained on Michael. How was she ever going to ask Michael if she couldn't even complete the thought to herself?

She started up the stairs, but stopped when she heard her mother's quick footsteps behind her.

"Vanessa, what were you going to tell me? What won't I believe?" Intense worry showed in her mother's eyes and her hands gripped the newel post as if she were afraid to hear what Vanessa had to say.

"Oh, that." Vanessa shrugged and searched her mind for a lie. "I'm worried about not getting accepted into UCLA."

Her mother's chest loosened as if she had been holding her breath. "It's too soon to worry about that." She smiled broadly. "Go on to bed now."

Vanessa nodded and continued up the steps to her room.

She had loved her bedroom once, but now the window seat where she had curled up to read, the thick white shutters, and the flowered wallpaper seemed to belong to someone else.

She wished Catty had spent the night so she could talk to her. Normally, they were inseparable, but lately Catty had been dividing her time between Vanessa and Tianna.

That brought up another problem. Vanessa knew she should feel closer to Tianna, but she hadn't been able to accept her as the others had. Catty, Jimena, and Serena had been born goddesses like Vanessa, but Tianna had become one after she had used her telekinetic powers to save the other four.

Instead of feeling grateful, Vanessa sometimes resented the way Catty and the others admired Tianna and spent so much time with her. She hated her negative emotions, but lately it seemed that they were consuming her, as if there were something bad inside her clawing to get out.

She sat at the keyboard that had belonged to her dad, slipped on the headset, and started picking out notes. Words flowed into her mind and slowly she put together lyrics that described the resentment, pain, and jealousy flowing through her. Her fingers found the right chords, and soon she had a melody. She stayed up for another hour, engrossed in her music. She didn't notice the wind rocking her window like a spirit demanding entrance.

CHAPTER THREE

THE NEXT MORNING, Vanessa bought a mocha Frappuccino at Starbucks on the way to school. She sipped the icy chocolate-coffee blend as she waited in line to go through the metal detectors at the front gate. The Santa Anas had cleared the air. Even the Hollywood sign in the hills behind her looked brighter, and with the line of palm trees around the campus and the turquoise sky, La Brea High looked like a post-card.

The day was too perfect to waste on school. She wished she had Catty's nerve. She'd love to ditch, but instead she handed her green straw purse to Mr. Bellows, the security guard.

"How are you, Vanessa?" Mr. Bellows smiled, exposing long teeth capped in gold, then opened her purse, glanced inside and handed it back to her.

"You didn't even check it," she complained.

"What would you have in there that I'd have to confiscate?" The idea made him chuckle. "I wish all the kids were like you."

"Yeah," Vanessa muttered and headed away. "Adults love me."

She stepped through the gate in the chain-link fence and crossed the blacktop. The cold drink was starting to give her an ice-cream headache. She pinched the bridge of her nose and bumped into two guys with perfect tans and waxed eyebrows.

"Hey, Vanessa." Tyler lifted his shades. He had a recurring role on *Days of Our Lives*. "Wanna help us with our sides?" He held up two pages of script with lines highlighted in blue.

"Not today," she answered with a smile. She

had helped them at other times. "I'm looking for Catty."

"There's a walk-on part for a gorgeous surfer blond." Emilio grinned, showing off dimples and dazzling white teeth. "You've got the look."

"Thanks, but I've got plans." She headed away, their voices following after her as they practiced their parts.

Many of her classmates were movie-star wanna-bes. Some even had agents and went on casting calls. They carried large duffel bags to school, filled with headshots and a change of clothes in case they got a last-minute call from their agents.

She climbed the front steps, weaving in and out of the heavy-metal kids who lounged on the steps in spiked collars and long hair. The hip-hop kids stayed on the other side of campus but Vanessa got along with everyone, even the scholars; kids like Serena who were taking classes at UCLA while they finished high school.

Vanessa looked back across the campus and wondered if the kids would still like her if she no longer tried to mold her personality to fit in. She wished she could do something radical that would shock everyone.

"Vanessa." Catty waved, then ran toward her, her arm extended to keep her coffee from spilling. She wore a see-through green top over a polka-dot bra and hip-hugging jeans that showed off the hoop piercing her belly button. When she got closer, Vanessa saw the blue paint stains on her wrist and thumb, and knew she'd been up late painting.

"I'm so glad I found you first." Catty's straight brown hair glimmered with coppery streaks. Her face had a natural glow. "You'll never guess what!"

"Tell me."

"The art department is entering one of my paintings in the school-district competition." Catty took a sip of coffee, her eyes watching Vanessa over the rim.

"That's great! Which one?" Vanessa asked.

"You haven't seen it yet."

"I haven't?" Vanessa was surprised. "I thought I'd seen everything."

"I used Tianna for my model this time," Catty explained.

"Oh." Vanessa could feel the smile slipping from her lips. "Why didn't you ask me?" Vanessa posed for Catty all the time. The goddesses in her paintings always resembled Vanessa.

"You were busy with Michael." Catty pulled yellow-tinted sunglasses from her messenger bag and slid them on.

"It's all right," Vanessa said, feeling hurt.

They walked in silence down the outside corridor toward Vanessa's locker. Finally Vanessa spoke. "Have you been having any trouble with your time traveling?"

Catty shook her head. "No, why?"

"I had trouble going invisible last night," Vanessa whispered.

"So what's new with that?" Catty laughed, then leaned closer so no one could hear. "A guy tries to kiss you, and you become as see-through as plastic wrap."

"True." Vanessa stopped in front of her locker. "But last night, I had a strange feeling after I became invisible, as if something was moving inside my cells."

Catty paused, pondering what Vanessa had said. "The Santa Anas ripped through everything last night." Catty tossed her cup in the trash. "Maybe there was too much sand and dust in the air. Our front yard was a mess this morning."

"You think that's all it was?" Vanessa opened her locker. "I hadn't closed the window. I guess it could have been the winds."

"Of course." Catty started to say more but before she could, the whoosh and tick of skateboard wheels riding over the seams in the sidewalk grew louder.

They turned. Tianna rode a skateboard toward them at breakneck speed. She shifted her weight, zipping in and out of kids walking to their classrooms. Her hooded jacket and funky jeans flapped against her. A duffel bag swung from her shoulder. Loose strands of her long silky black hair whipped into her eyes. She rarely bothered with makeup. She didn't need it.

"Hey." Tianna did a wheelie stop in front of

them, then picked up the skateboard and dropped it into the bag. Skateboards weren't allowed on campus.

"Tianna's got some big news, too." Catty seemed really excited. "They needed someone for the cheer competitions and asked Tianna to start practicing with them. She didn't want to at first, but of course, once she saw how dangerous it was, she couldn't resist. You should see her fly in the air."

"Catty should take the credit," Tianna answered modestly. "They never would have seen me perform if she hadn't taken me back in time to fill in after their captain got a stress fracture."

"We went back to last Friday's game," Catty added. "Tianna was so hot!"

Vanessa took out her Spanish book and slammed her locker shut with a loud clank.

"Don't act like you would have wanted to come." Catty seemed to pick up on Vanessa's emotions before she even understood them. "You hate the tunnel."

The tunnel was the hole in time they had to

travel through to get from one time to the next. Catty was right. Vanessa hated it, but she still felt a pinch of envy that they had done it without her.

"I knew you wouldn't want to go," Catty explained. "So I didn't ask. Besides, Tianna likes the tunnel."

"She does?" Vanessa wondered how anyone could. The air inside was too thick to breathe and the musty rotten-cabbage smell made her stomach turn.

Catty rested her arm on Tianna's shoulder. "She didn't even scream," Catty teased.

Vanessa raised an eyebrow. "How was the landing?"

"About as much fun as jumping from a speeding car." Tianna rolled up her sleeve to show a skinned elbow. "I didn't get this skateboarding."

"The landings are the worst," Vanessa agreed. Whenever they got to their time destination, they fell out of the tunnel with a hard crash. Vanessa had the bruises and broken sunglasses to prove it. She sighed. She hated everything about time traveling, so why did she miss it so much? And then she knew. She missed Catty.

Footsteps pounded behind her and then Derek was in front of them, his arm around Tianna. "Hey." He nodded a greeting, but his deep blue eyes never left Tianna. His red hair was twisted into dreadlocks and the sunburn on his nose made his freckles look darker. He pulled at his vintage tie-dyed T-shirt.

"I saw you turn a high ollie in the parking lot," Derek said to Tianna. "You gonna ditch me and turn professional?"

"No way. I like it best when it's just me, the street, and my board." Tianna tilted her head and gave Derek a sunshine smile. All the guys liked her, but she only liked Derek. She didn't have to be guarded with him.

"Gotta go. Meet me after school today," Derek yelled as he headed off again. "We'll go to the Ramp. I want to show you off." The Ramp was a legal skate park, but Vanessa knew Tianna liked skating steps, rails, and stairs in front of the offices on Wilshire.

"Can't tonight," Tianna shouted back. "Tomorrow." Tianna loved skating because she could take it as far as she wanted to go. Vanessa paused. She had never thought about it before, but that's the way she felt about her singing.

"Derek is such a cutie," Catty said, interrupting her thoughts.

Vanessa nodded as they started down the outside corridor toward class.

"Wait up!" Serena yelled from across the lawn that divided the rows of classrooms. She wore a short-cropped red shirt and the cutoff denim mini she'd made from her brother's cast-off jeans. The waist hugged her hips and revealed a slice of tanned skin as she walked toward them, carrying her cello case. Her hair, curled and long, bounced on her shoulders.

"Have you seen Jimena?" she asked, clinking her tongue ring against her teeth. "She called this morning and said to meet her at school. She had another premonition."

"There she is." Tianna motioned with her head.

"It doesn't look good," Catty murmured.

Jimena seemed breathless, as if she had run from the bus stop. Her curly black hair swung in the air behind her as she hurried to them. She wore baggy boot-camp jeans with green camouflage sneakers. A fringed short-sleeve T-shirt showed off the crescent moon and star Catty had tattooed on her arm. She also had two teardrops tattooed under her right eye—one from each stay in Youth Authority Camp—and a triangle of three dots on the web between her index finger and thumb.

"What did you see?' Serena whispered, and set her cello case near the bank of outside lockers.

"My friend Elena disappeared last night." She waited a moment to catch her breath before continuing. "She was working as a *mesera.*"

"A waitress?" Serena asked.

"Not exactly." Jimena shook her head. "Elena got hooked on taxi dancing."

Catty looked puzzled.

"At some of the clubs in the barrios, girls

charge a dollar to dance with a stranger," Jimena explained.

"You mean dancing for dollars?" Vanessa asked. "I didn't think that was real."

"Dancing with the guys for a few bucks is an easy way to make money and not as dangerous as stealing," Jimena explained. "So some of my homegirls lie about their age and go down there."

"How old are the guys?" Catty asked.

"Old enough to be your *abuelo*, maybe even your great-grandpa." Jimena went on, "But young guys go there, too. New immigrants from Mexico and Central America who miss their friends and family."

"That doesn't sound very safe." Vanessa thought it would feel creepy to dance with strangers for money.

"No es," Jimena agreed. "I've been warning them about it. And *la chota*, the cops, they've been trying to stop the fourteen- and fifteen-year-old girls from going down to the clubs, but it isn't easy." Jimena shook her head, her eyes troubled. "Elena, Leda, and Adriana went down to Heaven's

Ballroom. When it was time to leave, Leda and Adriana couldn't find Elena."

"Maybe we should call the police." Vanessa suggested. "She could have been kidnapped."

Jimena shook her head "Elena had told me that she met this *guapo* guy who looked like he was from a *telenovela*."

"So maybe she ran off with him," Serena said.

"No way. She wasn't like some naive little girl. She knew the score and didn't snap to it for the guys. Besides, in my premonition I saw Elena hugging some guy with glinting eyes."

"You think he was a Follower?" Tianna had a reason to hate Followers. They had broken into her house when she was a child and killed her parents and younger sister. Now she lived with a foster mother.

"Maybe, but—" Jimena paused as if she were considering. "There was a full moon last night, and Followers avoid going out then because their eyes glow and they can't blend in anymore. Elena wouldn't have trusted him even for one dance. In the premonition . . ." Jimena stared off as if she had seen something unbelievable.

Finally she looked back at them. "*Los ojos.* His pupils were burning, not just reflecting light. It was like I could see inside to his soul and it was on fire. He was something more than a Follower."

"You mean a Regulator, like Toby?" Vanessa asked. Regulators were so committed to the Atrox that their very appearance became distorted and twisted by its evil until they looked monstrous. But they also had the power to disguise themselves. Vanessa had been fooled into dating a Regulator named Toby.

Jimena shook her head.

The first bell rang, but they ignored it.

"I had always thought the stories told by the *viejas* were only folktales," Jimena began. "Something to keep the girls from going to the clubs, but now I wonder."

"What stories?" Tianna asked.

"It's a story about this smooth guy who can really dance and turn the girls' heads. He goes into the dance hall and all the *chicas* want to dance with him. He takes one into his arms and as she falls in love with him, she looks down, sees the flames beneath his feet, and knows he's the devil and that he's come for her soul."

"That's just an old superstition," Tianna said.

Jimena shrugged. "In some of the stories she looks down and sees the feet of a goat or a chicken but always it's the devil who is dancing with her. Sometimes she screams and the devil vanishes in a puff of smoke."

The corridor was empty now, except for a few kids running to class. A teacher began to lecture in the room behind them.

"You think the devil took your friend?" Catty whispered, her eyes wide.

Jimena nodded. *"Lo creo."*

"Let me look at the cards." Serena pulled her tarot pack from her backpack, knelt down on the sidewalk, and shuffled. She could read minds, but she could also sense things using her tarot deck. She never tried to force a meaning, but sometimes she caught glimpses of things to come.

She slapped the first card on the sidewalk in front of her.

Before Vanessa could see it, a sudden gust howled down from the sky and tore the cards from Serena's hands, scattering them in a circle.

Vanessa jumped for the Queen of Cups, but as her hand started to close around it, the wind thrashed through her fingers and snapped it away.

When Catty grabbed a handful of cards, a dusty funnel-shaped cloud whisked around her. She let the cards go and covered her eyes.

The major and minor Arcana coiled into a huge spiral and disappeared over the roof.

The wind died as quickly as it had come

"It's like the wind was alive," Catty said with awe.

One card fluttered back and landed in Serena's hand. She held it up. "The Devil," she whispered.

"You think it's a warning?" Vanessa asked in a low voice.

Serena nodded. "Something with tremendous power is trying to scare us away."

Tianna clenched her hands into fists. "I think we should look at the card as an invitation then," she said defiantly. "Let's go down to Heaven's Ballroom tonight."

They all nodded in agreement.

"Can you get your brother's car?" Serena asked.

"*Sin duda.*" Jimena didn't have a driver's license yet, but her brother let her use his car anyway. "I'll pick you up around ten. Meet at the usual places. Dress to kill."

Or be killed, Vanessa thought, staring at the Devil card in Serena's hand. Whatever waited for them at Heaven's Ballroom knew they were coming.

CHAPTER FOUR

AFTER SCHOOL, VANESSA sat on the concrete bench in the sunshine where she always waited for Catty and started her homework. The rhythm of the janitors' brooms sweeping out the classrooms filled the hot afternoon.

She was finishing her geometry homework when she heard the racket of kids leaving detention, and glanced up. Three guys bagged out in jeans and knee-length shirts strolled past her and nodded.

"Hi," Vanessa answered and glanced at her watch. It was five o'clock already. She had assumed Catty was working late in the art class, but maybe she had left school without Vanessa. Sadness filled her. Tianna had shattered their old routine. She imagined Catty had felt the same when Vanessa began seeing Michael. Vanessa had gathered her books and purse and started to leave, when she heard running footsteps and laughter.

She turned. Catty ran down the sidewalk toward her. The rumble of skateboard wheels drowned Catty's laughter as Tianna shot around the corner on her board, her knees moving from side to side to increase her speed. It looked like they were racing.

"Hi!" Vanessa shouted.

They stopped suddenly. Both looked surprised to see her.

"Hey," Catty called and walked over.

Tianna used her toe to flip her skateboard into her hand. The deck had been repainted with a moonscape. Vanessa wondered when Catty had done that.

"You waited for me?" Catty smelled of turpentine and linseed oil, as if she had just finished cleaning her brushes. Blue oil paint stained her green shirt and jeans. "Sorry. I thought you would have gone home by now."

"The sun felt good," Vanessa answered. "So I finished my homework."

"Great." Catty smiled too broadly. "Now I won't have to do it."

"You want to go over to my house?" Vanessa asked. "We can go through some of my mom's designs and pick out something to wear tonight."

Catty and Tianna exchanged quick glances, and Vanessa knew they were searching for an excuse.

"I have something to wear." Tianna balanced the skateboard on her shoulder. "It's not like I want to impress the guys we're going to see tonight anyway."

"We need to look the part." Vanessa glanced from Catty to Tianna and wondered why they were hesitating. Everyone liked to go through her mother's storeroom.

Catty played nervously with her beaded earring. Vanessa had known her long enough to know she was lying before she even spoke. "We have to research a report before we go out tonight."

"Yeah," Tianna agreed too quickly. "We have to go to the library."

Vanessa didn't bother to confront their lie. Catty never went to the library, and if there were a report due, Vanessa would know about it. Except for art, they had all the same classes.

"Okay." Vanessa masked her disappointment. "Another time."

"We'll walk you out to the bus stop." Catty's forced cheerfulness made anger burn inside Vanessa.

"I have to pick up something from the gym," Vanessa lied back. "I'll see you tonight."

"Yeah, we'll see you tonight then." Catty started walking with Tianna toward the front of the school.

"Right," Vanessa snapped.

Catty stared back at Vanessa, surprised at her tone.

"See ya." Tianna flipped her board onto the sidewalk, then nudged Catty.

They jumped on and tried to ride tandem. They took a few pushing steps together, then set their back legs on the deck at the same time. The skateboard rocked crazily from side to side, their squeals and laughter bouncing against the bank of lockers and echoing down the hall.

Vanessa turned and started toward the back of campus, the sun hot on her shoulders. She took a shortcut between the gym and the music building. Weeds brushed against her bare legs as she tromped over the crabgrass and dirt with short angry steps. Band practice had ended. The silence was so complete she could hear grasshoppers taking flight in front of her.

At the end of the narrow passage, she stopped and scanned the football field and bleachers. Usually someone was running track or passing a football, but today no one was there. Everyone was probably down at Venice Beach mixing with the in-line skaters and cyclists on the boardwalk. She wished she were there, diving into the cool water.

She walked along the side of the gym. Stored

heat from the day radiated from the beige stucco walls. Sweat beaded on her forehead. She started across the basketball courts, hoping for a breeze, but the blacktop was scorching and it felt as if the soles of her shoes were sticking to the tarry asphalt.

As she stepped onto the soccer field a strange feeling tickled the back of her neck. She felt as if someone were watching her. She studied the school yard. Heat waves rippled over the empty basketball courts. The sun had dropped lower, pushing long shadows from poles and palm trees across the soccer field, but she didn't see anyone.

She turned, anxious to be home, and started walking toward the student parking lot, her books clutched tight against her chest. She thought of the cold lasagna waiting for her in the refrigerator and then stopped abruptly. Something was wrong. She listened. She could no longer hear the twittering of birds or the traffic on La Brea. She suddenly wished she had gone with Catty and Tianna. For no reason she thought of the previous night and the feeling she had had of someone in the living room with her.

Almost as if her thought had conjured it, a sickeningly sweet fragrance floated around her. She took a quick step backward to escape the sudden gluey feel of the hot air. She remembered the taste of decay she had spit from her mouth the night before and she knew if she opened her mouth now, she would have that same unbearable taste on her tongue. Her heartbeat quickened and she glanced around her looking for the source of the smell.

Her eyes told her she was alone, but her body knew someone was nearby. She could feel it in her arms, neck, and back as if an unseen presence were stirring the air. She glanced down at her amulet. The sun reflected off the silver but it made no glow of its own.

She no longer cared who might see now. She released her molecules and soared upward before the change was even complete. She glanced down. Her speckled shadow slid over the grass and onto the student parking lot. Within seconds her shadow disappeared and she floated higher into the sultry air.

Something touched her like a snap of electricity. She darted away, but whatever it was caught up to her and stroked her head, as if it could see her. She jerked back, trying to see what it was, but the air around her was completely empty. She probed with her own molecules, hoping to touch it.

Immediately it closed around her, forcing its way through her with a prickling sensation. Escape was impossible now. It had tangled tightly around her, making her change direction.

If she materialized she might be able to get away, but that felt too risky. When she was a child, her molecules had sometimes come back together wrong. What would happen if she tried with this other thing fused within her cells? She might become hideously deformed—or worse, she might not be able to come back at all.

She struggled against it, and when she had control, she whirled precariously close to the ground, hoping to frighten whatever it was away.

When that didn't work, she jittered and shim-
mied, trying to shake free.

Then, abruptly, it was gone. Her molecules
slammed painfully together, and she fell to the
asphalt like a kid doing a belly flop. Her purse and
books scattered around her. She lay motionless on
the asphalt, the heat burning her cheek, and drew
in long thankful breaths. She hurt all over, but she
didn't think she had broken any bones.

She felt footsteps thundering across the
parking lot and jerked her head around.

"Vanessa!" Michael Saratoga waved at her.
He wore a tight blue short-sleeved shirt and faded
jeans with frayed hems and heavy black boots.

In moments he was next to her. He looked at
her in a way that made her feel as if he were seeing her for the first time. She breathed in his
clean, soapy smell and took his hand.

"You take a tumble?" he asked with a slow
easy smile. His thick black curls fell across his
face as he picked up her books and the lipstick
and mascara that had spilled from her purse, then
he stood, pulling her with him.

She closed her eyes, and rested her head against his chest, her knees still shaky.

He held her for a moment as if he understood. "It must have been quite a fall. Weren't you looking where you were going?" There was a lightness in his voice, but when she pulled back and looked at him she saw concern in his dark eyes.

She studied him, wondering if he had seen her become visible and fall from the air. He must have—but if he had, he definitely wouldn't act this calm. Maybe he had been looking in a different direction.

He took a Chapstick from his back pocket and rolled it over his lips.

She looked at him, surprised. She had never seen him use Chapstick before.

He misread her look and offered her the tube. "Want some?"

"No thanks."

"Cherry flavor." He rolled his tongue over his lips in a kidding way and pushed the Chapstick back in his pocket.

"I thought you weren't at school today," she asked, still staring into his dark eyes.

"Wasn't," he answered and started walking with her. "I thought you'd need a ride home."

"Yeah, thanks. How'd you know I'd be so late?"

"Didn't." He smiled. "But you weren't home, so I tried here."

The muscles in her back began to loosen. She couldn't resist the way he looked at her. Everything about him made her feel good. She glanced back at the school yard and wondered why she had felt so afraid moments before.

"What?" Michael asked and followed her look. "You see something?"

"Nothing," she answered, already convincing herself that her imagination had taken control again.

Michael put his arm around her. She liked him even more than she had when she first met him. She still got a sweet ache in her stomach when she saw him. It felt good. But in the beginning it had been bad, because every time she saw him, her molecules had started pinging out of control. She couldn't even remember now how many times she had almost gone invisible in front of him. She had wondered then if she'd ever be able to kiss him without becoming a ghost.

Now she wanted to take their relationship to another level. His hand smoothed up her side as if he sensed what she was thinking. Her heart raced, wondering if she should tell him her secret desire now. Why not? They were alone. She cleared her throat and started to speak. "Michael, I want to talk to you about—"

He tilted his head and in the slant of sunlight, she caught something in his eyes. They looked dark and tense.

"Is everything okay, Michael?"

"Sure. Why wouldn't it be?" he asked, and the smile returned to his eyes.

Maybe it had only been a reflection of the sun that had made her pause. "You looked different. That's all."

"New haircut." He shrugged and absently brushed his free hand through his hair. "And I had to borrow clothes from my cousin."

"Cousin?" She had never heard him mention his cousin before.

"You don't know him," he offered. "And I don't want to talk about him. I want to talk about us. We have plans to make. Your birthday is a few days away and you still haven't told me what you want to do."

She took a deep breath. She should just say it. She trusted Michael. She really liked him. She'd never felt this way about a guy before.

They crossed the student parking lot and when they reached the side street near the school Michael stopped in front of an old Chevy with red-and-orange flames running down its front fenders.

"Whose car is this?" she asked. Michael drove a Volkswagen bus that had belonged to his father in the sixties. It was still painted with psychedelic pink-and-orange flowers.

"Same cousin. It's a mess. Sorry."

The smells of stale French fries and hamburgers rushed from the hot interior when he opened the passenger's side door. Wadded fast-food wrappers filled the space under the glove compartment.

She settled in, watching him. His eyes lingered on her in a way they hadn't since their first date. She loved the way his lips curled around his perfect white teeth when he smiled the way he was now. What was it about him that made her like him so much? She smiled back at him before he slammed the door.

She rolled down the window and glanced around the inside of the car. Fake leopard fur covered the steering wheel and a silver skull with red eyes dangled on a chain from the rearview mirror.

Michael ran around the front of the car and climbed in behind the steering wheel. He grinned at her as he settled into the sheepskin-covered seat, then he unexpectedly grabbed her hand and pulled her toward him. He kissed her full on the lips.

"Sorry," he whispered as he pulled back.

"Michael, why are you sorry?" she asked. "About what?"

"I shouldn't have kissed you but I couldn't resist." He bent forward and turned the key in the ignition. The car filled with a heavy thump of rap music. His hand darted forward and turned off the radio.

"Shouldn't?" she asked, dismayed. She could see him blushing despite his dark skin, and then she realized why he looked so different. "You're not wearing your earring." She pulled at the collar of his shirt. "Or the charm your grandfather gave you."

He shrugged. "Forgot." He steered the car away from the curb. "Have you decided what you want for your birthday yet?" Michael asked, changing the subject.

"Go out, I guess."

"I want the celebration to be special for you," he said. "Anything. You name it. I'll make it happen."

She bit her lip, trying to find the words to

say what was on her mind. His hand reached over and took hers as if he sensed her turmoil.

"What?" he teased. "You only bite your lip when you have something important to say."

"I do," she considered. Maybe that was true.

"Tell me," he coaxed.

"I—" Her feet began to tingle. This was as bad as when she had first tried to kiss him. "I want to . . . I want you to . . ." she stopped. She felt heat rising to her cheeks. Any other guy wouldn't wait for his girlfriend to ask. Maybe Michael didn't like her enough.

She cleared her throat and started again even though her legs had started to become a dusty swirl.

"What?" he asked, his gorgeous eyes never leaving hers. "Just say it. I won't bite."

"I want . . ." Invisibility was dangerously near. She couldn't ask the question now. "I want you to stop at the market on the way home so I can get some Jelly Bellies."

He laughed. "That's all? Why were you so nervous to ask me that? I thought it was going to be something important." He seemed disappointed.

She stared off and wondered when she was going to have the nerve to tell him what she really wanted.

T HAT NIGHT, VANESSA slipped into the slinky red dress she had taken from her mother's storage room. It was low cut, slit up the side, and clung perfectly to her body. She sprayed musky cologne into the air, then whirled into the fragrance, hoping to cover the mothball and new-material smell of her outfit.

Standing in front of her bedroom mirror, she pulled on spiky black shoes, fluffed her curls and added rhinestone earrings. She studied her reflection, pleased with the glam look she saw.

At last, she hurried outside. Her heels clicked

on the sidewalk as she darted from shadow to shadow, hiding so neighbors couldn't see her and tell her mother.

Around the next corner Jimena was waiting for her, leaning against the hood of her brother's blue-and-white '81 Oldsmobile. She waved when she saw Vanessa and started toward the driver's side, twirling the keys around a finger. She wore a gold jacket over a shiny halter and a sparkling denim skirt. Her black hair shimmered in the streetlights.

The others were already in the car. Vanessa wondered why Jimena had picked them up first, but brushed the thought aside when Tianna opened the rear door and scooted over, her metallic pink skirt clinging to her thighs.

"Cool style." Vanessa complimented her hair as she crawled in.

Tianna had combed it into a French twist. The ends fanned out on top, and her bangs were spritzed with gloss and hanging in her eyes.

"You ready for this?" Catty asked, running her hands over her seductive black dress. "Can you imagine what our parents will do if they find out?"

Both Tianna and Catty were wearing impossibly high stacked heels.

"What are you going to do if we have to run?" Vanessa closed the car door and settled in.

"It's on you to make us invisible." Serena turned from the front seat and kicked a foot in the air, showing off spiked sandals with straps tied around her ankle. Her hair was pulled back tight, and her earrings swung to her shoulders.

Vanessa put her own foot up, turning her shoe. "I'm wearing ankle breakers, too."

They broke into laughter as Jimena turned the ignition. The mufflers thundered, and raucous music vibrated inside the car, ending conversation. She turned the steering wheel, then pressed her foot on the accelerator and they sped toward downtown.

Catty and Tianna waved their hands in the air, their upper bodies swaying to the beat. Vanessa bobbed her head, then closed her eyes and let the cool night breeze rush over her.

Twenty minutes later, Jimena turned off the

music. The silence made Vanessa's ears ring. She looked out the window as they sped through the Harbor Freeway underpass and buzzed by the L.A. Convention Center and the Staples Center. She caught a whiff of grilling steaks from the Pantry as Jimena made a quick left turn, followed by a right.

She drove slowly as she continued down a street lined with old brick apartments and hotels. At the next corner, women holding candles walked in a circle, their faces solemn in the candle glow. Two more, bundled in jeans and heavy jackets, ran across the street to join them.

Jimena put on the brakes and made a quick turn into a driveway, then backed out.

"What is it?" Vanessa asked.

Four old woman sat on the stoop beneath the flashing pink sign that read HEAVEN'S BALL-ROOM. The neon light strobed over their wrinkled faces as they fingered the beads of their rosaries, lips moving in unison.

"Some of the women from the community are holding a candlelight vigil in front of the club," Jimena explained. "They're upset about Heaven's Ballroom allowing minors to dance for money. I should have know they'd be down here, since Elena didn't come home."

"Are we leaving, then?" Vanessa asked.

"Not a chance." Jimena pulled into an alley.

The car bumped over the ruts in the road, then swung wildly as Jimena parked between a rusted pickup and a silver Mercedes. She braked and shut off the ignition.

"The mothers out front think they're stopping the guys from going into the ballroom." Jimena shook her head. "They haven't figured out yet that everyone sneaks around to the back when they're blocking the door."

"How do you know so much about it?" Serena asked.

"How do you think?" Jimena slid from the car and slammed the door.

Catty and Tianna climbed out but Vanessa stayed behind, watching Jimena through the front windshield as she walked to the back stairs. Everyone had heard about Jimena's gang-girl reputation, and she had the scars and tattoos to prove it. But Vanessa felt sorry for her. No matter how tough she might be, jacking cars and dancing for dollars had to be scary when you were only twelve years old.

A fuzzy feeling crossed her mind, and she glanced up. Serena was looking at her.

"Reading my thoughts?" Vanessa smiled back at her.

Serena nodded. "Just don't let Jimena catch you feeling sorry for her."

The others were already climbing the stairs. Vanessa ran to catch up, stepping carefully around broken beer bottles, Serena close behind her.

At the top of the stairs Vanessa read a hand-painted sign, HOSTESS DANCING, before pushing inside.

A man with a potbelly sat at the door, his orange-blond hair slicked away from his face with too much pomade. He licked his thumb when he saw them and counted out five manila cards, then handed them each one. He had a large gold ring on every finger, including his thumb.

"Punch your time card before you start to dance." He pointed to a metal box with a clock in its center, hanging on the wall. "That's how you get paid. Make the men pay to talk and sit with you, too, and don't think watching TV comes without paying, but they get to look all they want for free." He laughed as if he had told them a joke.

When none of them laughed back, he waved them inside, the diamonds in his rings sparkling.

Holding her time card tightly, Vanessa followed the others into the ballroom. They stopped in front of a big sign, painted in large red letters, that read GIRLS ARE NOT ALLOWED TO LEAVE THE CLUB WITH A CUSTOMER DURING WORK HOURS.

A disco ball whirled from the ceiling, casting dappled light across the room. Women danced with their purses over their shoulders, others held their time cards tight between their fingers. The ones who weren't dancing crowded into red booths on one side of the room, tapping their cards nervously on the tabletops. Most of them wore short, tight, low-cut dresses, but some were wearing jeans and halter tops.

Across the room old men in suits sat at tables drinking beers and gazing at the women. They pointed and talked freely, analyzing the women's looks and bodies in loud voices.

Tianna let out a long whistle, staring at a bent-over man with a long thin nose and yellowed white hair. "Some of these guys are old geezers."

Vanessa glanced at Tianna. It was the first time she had ever seen her look unsure.

"Why do you think these old guys come here?" Jimena asked. "It's make-believe. They pretend they're young and that you've got a big crush on them. You work on that and you can make fifty dollars *sin duda*." Jimena's smile was more of a sneer.

"You better stop staring at him." Catty teased Tianna. "He probably thinks you want to dance with him."

As if on cue, the old man scraped his chair away from the table, hitched up his gray slacks, and started walking toward Tianna with a toothless grin.

"I'm outta here." Tianna turned to go.

Jimena caught her elbow. "You're investigating. ¿*Sabes?* Punch in the card when he asks you to dance and talk about Elena."

A fast-moving song from the sixties came on.

"Hit it." Catty whooped and started dancing with sinuous moves like a cat against Tianna. "Show him what you got, Tianna," Catty teased. "I hope Derek won't be jealous."

Vanessa knew Catty was only trying to cheer everyone up, but Jimena seemed annoyed.

"You don't dance without a guy," Jimena said and looked back at the bouncers talking to the manager at the door. "You wanna get us kicked out?"

"So arrest me," Catty said and kept moving.

"It's not funny." Tianna's muscles tensed as the man's gnarled hand reached out.

He grabbed Catty's wrist. She stopped dancing, her mouth dropped open and she stared at his wrinkled face inches from hers.

"Go dance with him, Catty," Tianna said, teasing back. "I know you were hoping he'd ask you."

He bowed gallantly, his brown tie falling in front of him. "You dance nice," he said, escorting Catty to the metal box.

Catty turned and mouthed *Help!* as she punched in her card.

The man pulled Catty tight against him and they marched across the floor, cheek-to-cheek, arms stretched out, doing something that looked like a tango.

"How can girls do this?" Serena whispered.

"They need the *dinero*." Jimena looked around the room. "Don't be afraid of the old men. And the young guys are just a bunch of lonely *braceros*, you know, day laborers, but back in their own countries they were probably accountants and businessmen. You pay a big price to come to the U.S. of A. I see Adriana."

Jimena started across the dance floor toward a girl dressed in glitter slacks, standing alone against the wall, her arms wrapped protectively around her. Her eyes looked red, as if she had been crying, and mascara streaked down her cheeks. When she saw Jimena, she started walking toward her with brisk steps, her hands wiping at her face.

"*¿Qué te pasa?*" Jimena placed a comforting arm around Adriana's shoulder.

"Leda disappeared." She stifled a sob.

"Why'd you come down here after I told you not to?" Frustration rose in Jimena's voice.

Adriana frowned and her eyes looked shiny. "We thought we'd be safe if we stayed together, but then . . ." Her lower lip quivered and she bit it.

"What?" Jimena asked impatiently.

"Leda went to the rest room, and when she came back she told me she was going to meet this guy out back—"

"You told her not to go—"

"*Claro,* but you know Leda. So when I saw her leave, I followed her."

Jimena nodded.

"But she wasn't there." Adriana raised her eyebrows as if she couldn't believe what she was saying.

"Did you go look for her?" Jimena asked.

She shook her head. "*Escucha.* You're not

understanding what I'm saying." Adriana's voice became a dry whisper. "I saw her go out the door and I followed her too quickly not to be able to see her walking down the steps, *pero se ha esfumado.* She vanished."

Vanessa noticed the fine tremor in Leda's hands as she scraped her fingers through her glossy black hair.

"You didn't see the guy?" Serena asked.

Adriana shook her head. "You can't see the devil unless he wants you to see him."

An accordion-based *norteño* started up, and a handsome man wearing a starched *guayabera* shirt tapped Jimena's shoulder. He didn't look much older than she was.

"What?" She looked at him oddly.

He held out a callused hand. "Dance?"

A strange look crossed Jimena's face, as if she had forgotten why they had come. She reached behind her, grabbed Tianna's arm, and pulled her forward. "I've got to take my friend home, but Tianna will dance with you."

Tianna blushed. She started to turn, but

caught Jimena's warning look and instead forced a big smile on her face. "Hi," she said and walked over to the gray clock on the wall and slipped in her card as if she had been dancing for dollars for ages. Then, with a hop, she started dancing something that looked like a polka.

"I'm going to take Adriana home." Jimena took the keys from her pocket. "Will you guys be okay until I get back?"

Vanessa nodded as Catty joined them, her face flushed from dancing, her clothes smelling of the old man's cologne.

"This is too much," Catty muttered. "Maybe we should all leave."

Jimena put her hands on her hips, but her face looked as if she were going to laugh. "You've fought Followers, but now you're going to let a bunch of lonely men scare you away?"

"I didn't imagine it'd be like this," Catty said. "You said 'old', but I didn't think you meant *old*."

"Just pretend it's your prom." Jimena started walking away with Adriana. "Serena, you come with me, *chica*."

Serena started after them.

Vanessa sighed and looked to the back of the club. "We'd better check it out."

"I don't think we're going to find anything." Catty walked with her, pushing through the couples on the dance floor. The women smiled at the men, but when they looked at each other frowns pinched their faces.

The music seemed quieter in the back. A few couples snuggled on couches watching the Lakers game. Catty nudged Vanessa, who followed her gaze. In a dark corner a couple was kissing, the girl clutching a time card in the her hand. She looked their age.

"I feel like going out front and lighting a candle," Vanessa whispered.

"Yeah." Catty nodded. "After tonight I deserve to finally get a nose ring."

"I can't believe you haven't done that yet." Vanessa glanced at the canteen. A woman with dyed red hair and penciled eyebrows poured a can of Pepsi into glass. "What are you waiting for?"

Catty shrugged. "I know it sounds silly, but

I kind of want to wait until I have something special to celebrate."

Vanessa laughed as they walked back to the dance floor past a line of young men who didn't bother concealing their stares.

"You think this is what it feels like to be in a beauty contest?" Catty asked as a hand grabbed her shoulder. She rolled her eyes, then smiled at the thin young man behind her, took her time card, and punched in before she started dancing.

Vanessa sat in a booth, anxious to leave. She watched the back door for Jimena and Serena to return.

The door opened and a young man walked inside wearing a western yoke shirt and a wide-brimmed white cowboy hat. The gold bead on the chin strap dangled below his square chin. His polished boots reflected the light as he stepped to the manager and handed him some bills. He removed his cowboy hat, creasing the center carefully. His bangs fell into his eyes, giving him a mysterious look. He glanced around the dance floor as if searching for someone, then his dark eyes stopped on Vanessa.

She felt embarrassed that he had caught her looking at him but she didn't look away—something in his gaze held her. He stood taller than Michael by maybe three inches, and he couldn't have been much older—eighteen at the most.

He started walking through the dancers toward her.

She jerked her head away, slunk deeper into the booth, and tapped the table with her fingernails as if she were engrossed in the music.

He stopped in front of her, his hand sliding under her chin. "Do you wish to dance with me?" The cadence of his English was odd, but she couldn't place the accent.

She looked up, too stunned to speak. He was incredibly handsome, but he didn't have that cocky tilt of the head that some guys developed when they knew they had killer looks.

"Well?" His smile revealed straight white teeth and dimples in both his cheeks. Her stomach seemed to drop. She had heard girls at school talk about falling in love at first sight, but she had never believed in it. If anything, it was infatuation, not love, but as heat rose up her neck she wondered if it could be true.

She took his hand, her heart hammering and wiggled from the booth, cursing the shortness of her dress and the low neckline, but at the same time feeling seductive and daring.

"I've never seen you here before." His hand gently touched her waist as she walked over to the time clock.

"First time," she said, pushing her time card into the metal box. It made a loud stapling sound and then she pulled it out.

"I'm glad I found you before someone else did." He took her hand, pulling her into his arms.

Vanessa smiled, amazed at the way he pretended they had just met at a dance. She breathed in the smell of his freshly laundered clothes, then felt something on his chest and glanced down. A box of Good and Plenty stuck out from his shirt pocket.

He caught her look, pulled out the box, and

rattled the white and purple candies into his palm. "Do you want some?"

She shook her head.

He threw them into his mouth and chewed vigorously, the smell of licorice filling the air around her.

"They're good." He didn't seem embarrassed by the black stains gathering around his teeth. Or maybe he didn't care because he was paying her to be with him. She didn't mind. She liked the uninhibited way he was enjoying the candy.

"You're eating like you've never tasted them before." She laughed.

"We don't have them where I come from." He slipped the box back in his pocket and took her hand.

"Where's that?" she asked.

He ignored her question and asked one of his own. "I've been searching for someone for a long time. Have you also?"

She glanced up at him. "You mean Elena and Leda?"

He seemed confused. "I mean you. I saw you

and thought I was seeing someone I had lost a long time ago."

Her heart sank. She remembered what Jimena had said about this being make-believe. He must be practicing lines on her or trying to relive a favorite memory.

"Is that why you looked at me so oddly?" she asked, noticing the diamond stud in his ear.

"I saw you staring at me when I walked in," he said. "And I had hoped that you had been searching for someone like me. Do you believe in love at first sight?"

Vanessa felt a blush rising to her cheeks again. Pretend, she thought. It's only a fantasy. But her emotions felt real. How could she like someone so quickly?

"Yes," she murmured, glancing into his eyes. She knew she should be asking him questions about Elena and Leda, but her mind wasn't on investigating. She suddenly wanted to kiss him, though she knew it was wrong. She didn't even know his name.

"Hector," he whispered against her ear.

She pulled back, surprised. "Why did you tell me your name?"

"I was introducing myself," he answered. "Didn't you want to know my name? I want to know yours."

She felt flustered and foolish. "Vanessa," she said, thinking she should have lied and given him a different name.

"Be my date, Vanessa?" His voice sounded sincere.

"Date?" She felt confused now, wondering if the question had a double meaning she didn't understand.

"Don't dance with anyone else tonight, only me." He nuzzled against her and she didn't mind the feel of his cheek pressed against hers. "Let me pretend for a few hours at least that you belong to me. You look like the kind of girl who gets lots of telephone calls and invitations."

"I guess as many as anyone at school."

"You go to school?" He seemed surprised, and then she remembered that she was underage and shouldn't be in Heaven's Ballroom.

Her instinct was to lie, but when she looked in his eyes, she found herself nodding. "La Brea High."

His hand reached up and caressed her hair. She started for a moment, unsure, but she enjoyed his touch.

"You must be very popular," he said softly.

"I try to be liked by everyone," Vanessa confessed. "I do a lot to fit in."

"We all do," he agreed. "But let's make a pact that we'll always tell each other the truth. Tell me your deepest secret."

Did she dare tell him? She knew you were never supposed to talk about another boyfriend on a date, but this wasn't a real date and it wasn't like she was ever going to see him again. Before she had even thought it through, the words rushed from her mouth. "I want more from my relationship with Michael, but I can't bring myself to ask him because I'm afraid he'll think I'm being too forward and then what if he says no?"

"Who is Michael?" he asked, his eyes

looking at her with a hint of jealousy. Was that part of the masquerade, too?

"He's my boyfriend," she answered finally.

He nodded with full understanding. "If I were your boyfriend, you'd never have to ask. I would know what you wanted."

She smiled, trying to remind herself that he was paying her to dance with him. This was only practice for him. So why were her emotions so involved? She liked him and that worried her. How could she like two guys at once? But she wanted to see Hector again.

Then another thought came to her, if she was careful, no one would even know she was seeing him. This part of town was far away from where she lived. She wouldn't have to worry about her reputation or what kids might think. No one was ever going to know.

She bit her lip. Could she really sneak behind Michael's back and date someone else? She'd never thought she was that kind of girl, but lately she had been discovering that she was different from the person she had always thought she was.

CHAPTER SIX

THE DANCE FLOOR was crowded now. The air conditioner blew cold air across the room but did little to relieve the heat from so many bodies. The waitress in the canteen made popcorn, the aroma mingling with the smells of perfume, beer, cigarette smoke, and sweat.

Vanessa leaned against Hector, enjoying the feel of his body next to hers. When the music changed they did quick salsa steps as if they had been dancing together for years.

Jimena tapped Vanessa's shoulder. "Come on. We're going to leave."

Vanessa glanced up at Hector. "I have to go," she said in a dreamy whisper and pulled away from him. She handed him her time card to let him know she wasn't going to turn it in and get paid for the evening they had spent together.

He seemed unhappy to let her go, but he didn't take her card and he didn't ask for her telephone number. She had the impression that he wanted to kiss her, but he didn't.

"Well, see you." She shrugged, disappointed, and hurried across the wood floor, weaving in and out of the fast-moving couples.

When she caught up to Jimena, she asked, "What's up?"

"Serena did a mind read on every guy here." Jimena looked defeated. "And none of them know anything about Elena or Leda."

"Where is Serena now?" Vanessa glanced back across the room and as she did, she realized she wasn't searching for Serena; she was checking to make sure Hector hadn't asked another girl to dance. Why should she care?

It wasn't like she was ever going to see him again. But she did care. And that troubled her.

"She's waiting out in the car with a big *dolor de cabeza*," Jimena said. "She's got one fat headache. She didn't pick up any good thoughts from these guys. They were thinking about the women like they were buying used cars."

Jimena slammed through the door, but before Vanessa left, she turned, straining to see Hector one last time. He glanced at her, with a slight smile. She started to wave, but Jimena pushed back inside, grabbed her hand, and pulled her out on the landing.

The door shut behind them, making the music seem far away.

Jimena shook her head and crossed her arms over her chest. "You were hoping that guy would come running after you and ask for your telephone number."

"I was not," Vanessa lied and started down the stairs.

"Forget him," Jimena said quietly.

"Like I need to forget him," Vanessa said, throwing her time card over the railing.

"I saw that look in your eyes," Jimena said. "Guys will tell girls anything to get them to snap to it."

"Hector's not like that." Vanessa grabbed hold of the splintered handrail, wondering why she was defending Hector. She barely knew him.

"You're getting played," Jimena said, her footfalls tapping behind them.

"I am not." Vanessa felt anger rising inside her but if she thought about it, she knew Jimena was right, yet her emotions were pulling her in the opposite direction. She stopped. "Okay, maybe I am."

"What you did here tonight wasn't real," Jimena said as they walked down the alley, kicking through yellowed newspapers and orange peelings, toward the car. "It's one big pretend in there, and if you let your emotions get involved you'll end up hurt bad."

"I know that," Vanessa said with a sigh. "It's just that he didn't know me, and it gave me a chance to express parts of myself that I hadn't realized were there before."

"*Ya lo vi.* I saw you acting like your evil twin." Jimena laughed, circling an arm around Vanessa, and leaned her head against her. "A few years back maybe I would have even jumped you into my gang. You would have made one badass home-girl."

Now Vanessa laughed. "I acted that bad?"

Jimena shook her head. "Nah, you'll never be bad enough for my old *klika*. You're too sweet and nice." Then her tone changed. "I wish we could have found Elena and Leda."

"Me, too. What happens to the girls in the folktales?" Vanessa asked when they reached the car. "The ones who don't scream and make the devil disappear?"

Jimena opened the car door and looked at her. "They never come back."

"We'll find your friends," Vanessa said and crawled into the rear seat next to Tianna.

Jimena started the engine and backed up, then shifted into drive, and the car spun away, spraying gravel from the back tires. She turned on the music, and the booming vibrations set off car alarms, leaving a trail of beeping horns and synthetic noise as they drove back to Hollywood.

Vanessa thought of Hector on the way home. Words floated in her mind and she started composing the lyrics for another song, a wailing bittersweet ballad about impossible love. She wanted to make the music dynamic and cathartic. Already, she could feel her fingers aching to find the keys, but she didn't say anything. She hadn't told any of them about her new passion. She was too afraid they'd laugh.

She wondered what her onstage presence would be. Some of the singers she saw had her wholesome look but they were intense and earthy when they sang. She didn't know if she'd have the courage. She might be too embarrassed to show her most private thoughts in public, but she'd have to try someday.

When the car stopped she looked up, surprised to see they were parked in front of her house.

"Why are you letting me off first?" she asked. "It's out of the way."

"I just got driving and forgot where I was," Jimena answered, glancing at Vanessa in the rearview mirror.

"Right." Vanessa slid out and slammed the door.

The car blasted away before she had even stepped on the curb. She watched the rear end fishtail around the corner. She had a strange feeling that if she became invisible and went over to Jan's Café in a few minutes, she'd find them gathered around a table, discussing their next move. She started to go invisible and stopped. She didn't want to spy on them. She wanted to work on her music.

With quick steps, she started up the front walk. She had forgotten to turn on the porch light again, and in the darkness the twisted olive tree looked like a monster ready to pounce. She hurried around to the back, singing the melody for her new song and reworking the words, anxious to go upstairs to her keyboard before she lost the arrangement she was imagining.

But as she neared the corner of the house, she stopped. A sharp sense of impending danger made her nerves thrum. She listened. A thumping sound came from the back. She crept forward and peered into the yard, scanning the patio with its broken cover, the hibiscus bush, and planters. Then she saw the door that led to the utility room.

It was open, swinging on its hinges, the breeze knocking it against the side of the house. She didn't think her mother could have forgotten to shut the door. She was too careful.

Vanessa tiptoed toward the banging door, afraid someone might be lurking behind the trees. A sudden rapping sound on the window upstairs startled her. She jumped back, pressing against the trunk of a cottonwood, and glanced up.

A face appeared in her bedroom window, and then it was gone. Her heartbeat quickened as new worry spread through her. Maybe the intruder from the night before hadn't been her imagination after all and her mother was now inside, needing her help.

She hurried up the back steps and into the utility porch, her feet tapping loudly on the linoleum. She slipped from her shoes, leaving them by the washer, and continued barefoot into the kitchen.

In the dark her mother's worktable, piled high with swatches of cloth and sketches, seemed unfamiliar. The shadows took on monstrous shapes. She glanced into the living room. Nothing looked out of place, but instinct told her there was something dangerous in the house with her. She glanced down at her moon amulet. It was not glowing, but her nerves were on fire, warning her of another presence.

She tried to turn invisible and go upstairs to investigate but her molecules refused to respond. Her cells knit together in frozen panic.

She stepped into the living room, her hands trembling, and squinted at the stairs, then started across the hardwood floor and stopped.

A low rustling came from the top of the stairs like the soft sound of pant legs brushing against each other when someone walked. She thought of the face in the window and wondered if her mother had run to her bedroom to hide from a prowler.

Before Vanessa was even aware of what she was doing, her feet were hitting the stairs, taking them two at a time. She bounded down the hallway and threw open the door to her mother's bedroom.

"Mom?"

The room was empty. She wondered what she had expected to see.

She ran into the hallway again, adrenaline pumping through her, and bolted into her room. She stopped abruptly at the door, holding back a scream. What she saw made her heart stop.

CHAPTER SEVEN

CATTY SAT IN THE chair beside Vanessa's bed, her hair and clothes looking as if she had been blown through a sandstorm. Smudges of soot and dirt covered her face and blood trickled from her lip. Worse was the expression in her eyes. She seemed terrified.

"What happened?" Vanessa felt confused, wondering how Catty had changed her appearance so quickly. Then she saw the nose ring and knew that this Catty was not the one she had said good-bye to only moments before.

"Let me see your hands." Catty spoke hurriedly.

Vanessa held them up, stretching her fingers. "What is it? What's wrong? You look terrible. Did someone hurt you?"

"No, I have to warn you." Catty seemed to be struggling against some force that Vanessa couldn't see.

"About what?" Vanessa asked.

A black void appeared in the air behind Catty. It was the tunnel she used to travel from one time to the next. Catty's head jerked around and from the shocked look on her face, Vanessa was positive she hadn't been the one to open it.

"Help me stay!" Catty yelled, scrambling away from the tunnel and grasping the edge of the bed.

Vanessa ran to her and tried to grab her arm, but before she could, Catty was yanked back and sucked into the darkness behind her. She shrieked as Vanessa lunged forward, trying to catch her leg. Her fingers started to close around Catty's ankle, but the tunnel shut with a whip of stinging air. A roar and burst of white light filled the room, and the tunnel was gone.

Vanessa fell, landing on her stomach, her arm twisting painfully under her.

The room was silent again but an odd sulfurous smell hung in the air, as if the tunnel had brought something back from the future when it had opened and pulled Catty inside.

Vanessa sat up, coughing, and waved at the thin veil of smoke.

If Catty had made this journey back in time to see her, then something must be desperately wrong, but what?

A loud noise in the hallway made Vanessa turn.

"Catty?" She ran from her bedroom and glanced both ways. "Catty?" she called again.

Vanessa had traveled with Catty enough times to know she seldom had precise landings. They frequently landed miles from their destinations. Catty might have planned to come back to Vanessa's room, but Vanessa doubted she could be that accurate.

She opened the door to the bathroom, expecting to see Catty sprawled on the tile floor.

Instead, the bathroom was empty; she turned back to the hallway and saw something odd.

A flame twisted across the carpet runner like a snake. At least she thought it was a small blaze. She bent over and touched it. It didn't feel hot. She picked it up and held it in her palm. It wiggled around, flapping like any normal fire, but it didn't cast any light.

She cupped her hands and examined the flame more closely. Without warning, it wrapped around the third finger of her left hand, burning into her flesh.

"Ouch!" She shook the flame free and jumped back. It vanished before touching the floor.

She hurried back to the bathroom and ran cold water over her wound, then examined the blister circling her ring finger.

She needed to talk to Catty. She went to the phone in her room and punched the speed-dial button for Catty's home phone. When the answering machine picked up she tried Catty's cell phone. No luck there either.

Finally, she put the receiver back in its cradle and plopped on her bed, studying the burn. Had Catty brought the flame with her from the future? Was it part of the warning?

CHAPTER EIGHT

SUNSHINE AWAKENED Vanessa with the promise of a hot day. She moussed her hair as she walked to the bathroom, then, bending at the waist, flipped her head upside down and turned on the blow-dryer. When she was finished drying her hair, she flung her head back and used a curling iron to make spirals. She held the top pieces of hair back with butterfly barrettes, put on makeup, and dressed in cotton slacks and a funky crocheted top with smiling flowers stitched across the front. She slipped into sandals, grabbed her straw purse, and hurried downstairs and outside, anxious to get to Catty's house before she left for school.

Morning mist was still clinging to the Hollywood Hills when Vanessa stood under the wind chimes on Catty's porch, knocking on the front door. A hummingbird darted around her, then flew to the pink oleander blossoms swaying near the redwood fence.

In a few seconds, Catty opened the door, a glazed doughnut in her hand. "Vanessa!" She looked surprised to see her and it made Vanessa feel sad; just a short time ago her visits were expected.

"I have to talk to you." Vanessa stepped inside. The room smelled of sandalwood incense and morning coffee.

Tianna peeked from the kitchen and waved, a spatula in her hand. "Hi, Vanessa."

"What's wrong?" Catty asked, concern covering her sleepy face.

"Last night you came back to my house." Vanessa sat on the cushion Catty's mother used to sit on when she meditated.

Catty looked at her oddly. "I came here last night. I didn't even call you."

"I mean you visited me from the future, and you looked frightened, as if something really bad had happened."

Catty stuffed the rest of the doughnut in her mouth and sat on the cushion next to Vanessa. "Are you sure I came from the future?" She licked her fingers. "It could have been a visit from the past when I was trying to improve the distance I could travel."

"No," Vanessa said. "You had a nose ring."

"Really?" Catty seemed excited. "Did it look good?"

Vanessa frowned.

"Sorry," Catty muttered. "Why did I come back from the future?"

"You said you had to warn me about something but before you could tell me what the danger was you were sucked back into the tunnel."

Catty started laughing.

"It wasn't funny." Vanessa felt irritation rising inside her. "It was really spooky."

"Sorry," Catty said through her giggles. "I have a confession to make."

"Yeah?" Vanessa waited for Catty to stop laughing.

"A couple of times when I've gotten really upset with you because you wanted to do your homework instead of hang out with me, I've thought about traveling into the past and making up some big warning to scare you."

"Why?"

"So you'd be too scared to be alone," Catty answered. "I thought maybe you'd call me then and beg me to come over because you'd want company. Sorry."

"You sure?" Vanessa asked, wondering if Catty was telling her the truth. "You looked ter-rified."

"Sure I'm sure." Catty winked. "I'll probably visit you again in a few days and tell you it was all a joke."

Vanessa stared at her, uncertain. "But why did you come back last night?"

Catty shook her head. "I probably got the

wrong night. It's not as if I don't make mistakes all the time."

Still Vanessa hesitated.

"Okay, it's childish. Asinine. I get the prize for a stupid use of my powers. I didn't mean to scare you." She tilted her head. "Forgive me?"

"It seemed so real." Vanessa considered. "If that was a put-on, you're a great actress."

"Of course I can act. I live in Tinseltown." Catty stood and started back to the kitchen. "Come on, let's eat breakfast. Tianna says she can make killer blueberry pancakes."

By noon, the heat had made the air sticky. Vanessa threw her books in her locker and hurried to meet her friends. They were going to walk to Pink's for hot dogs. Serena, Tianna, Jimena, and Catty stood in line at the front gate fanning themselves with their off-campus passes.

When Vanessa joined them, their conversation stopped abruptly, and they looked at her with red-faced grins. She didn't need to be a mind reader to know their blushes hadn't come from the heat; they had been talking about her.

"Hi," Serena said, sounding nervous. What had she been saying that she didn't want Vanessa to hear?

"What were you talking about?" Vanessa asked.

"Nothing." Serena seemed flustered, but Jimena started walking toward the security guard.

"*¡Andale!*" Jimena called over her shoulder. "Let's get moving. I'm starved."

"Did Jimena have a premonition about me?" she asked Catty.

"No." Catty shook her head. "Why would you think that?"

"Because it was so obvious you were talking about me," Vanessa said.

"We were not," Catty argued. "Get your pass out so we can leave."

Vanessa fumbled in her purse, but instead of retrieving her pass, she pushed it under her makeup bag. "I guess I forgot it," she lied. "You guys go on without me."

She started to walk away when Serena grabbed her hand, pulling her back.

"Hey!" Serena whistled admiringly. "Where did you get this cool henna tattoo?"

"What henna tattoo?" Vanessa glanced down and with a shock realized that the burn no longer looked like a blistering wound. It had spread, and now curled in a delicate floral design around her finger. She jerked her hand away from Serena and studied the paisley shape in the center of her palm. Her heart raced.

"That is so awesome," Tianna yelled. "I want one, too."

"I wish you had told me," Catty joined in. "I would have gone with you to get one." Then she looked at her curiously. "You didn't have it this morning. I would have noticed."

Vanessa searched her mind for an answer. She felt too nervous to tell them about the flame. Besides, it was probably some magician's trick that Catty had brought with her from the future. She was forever doing things like that to get Vanessa into trouble. She had before Tianna came into the picture, anyway.

"That's what they do to brides in India." Serena lifted her sunglasses to get a better look. "On her wedding day her friends cover her hands with a beautiful design like this one. It must have taken hours."

"Aren't you going to tell us where you got it?" Tianna asked.

"It's for the movie my mom is working on," Vanessa lied. "The woman who did it is in the makeup department." Then she looked at Catty, expanding her story. "I guess you didn't notice it this morning. Mom's friend did it before I left for school."

Vanessa took a deep breath, studying her friends. They seemed to believe her, and she didn't feel Serena tickling inside her mind.

After they left, Vanessa looked at her, hand again. The design baffled her, but she was more concerned with what her friends had been talking about. She stared through the chain-link fence, watching them and wondering if Jimena had had a premonition about her. Jimena's forewarnings always seemed to be about something bad, and the Daughters had never been able to stop any of them from coming true. Still, she'd rather know what was going to happen to her than have them keep it from her.

After school, Vanessa didn't wait for Catty on the bench. She was determined to get some answers. She went looking for Catty and found her carrying a large canvas covered with a white cloth.

"Is that the one you're entering in the district art contest?" Vanessa asked when she caught up to her.

Catty nodded and removed the cloth.

A full moon shimmered over the ocean as a goddess draped in billowing white robes emerged from a cresting wave. Her dark hair spiraled into the sea spray. The face definitely belonged to Tianna.

"You like it?" Catty asked.

Vanessa nodded. "It's the best you've ever done."

"Thanks." Catty covered the canvas and the two of them started walking again.

"So why did the conversation stop when I joined you guys earlier today?" Vanessa asked at last.

Catty stopped and looked at Vanessa, her face puzzled.

"You know what I mean," Vanessa confronted her. "You were so obviously talking about me. What was everyone saying?"

"No one was talking about you," Catty insisted, but the blush rising to her cheeks gave Vanessa a different answer.

"What's going on?" Vanessa couldn't keep the anger from rising in her voice.

"Nothing," Catty snapped and started walking again, her steps quick.

"It's not as if I don't know." Vanessa hurried beside her. "Even last night something was up. Jimena never drops me off first."

"Can't you ever stop worrying about what other people think about you?" Catty readjusted the painting and looked away from her. "You shouldn't be so paranoid."

"I'm not talking about other people," Vanessa corrected her. "I'm talking about my best friends. Did Jimena have a premonition that the rest of you are keeping from me?"

Catty's head whipped back. "No!" she insisted. "It's your imagination."

"It's not—" Before Vanessa could finish her sentence, Tianna and Derek joined them.

"Show Derek the painting." Tianna carried a helmet and elbow protectors in one hand, her skateboard in the other.

Catty removed the cloth.

Derek whistled and set his skateboard on the ground. "Awesome. It really looks like Tianna." He brushed back a dreadlock that had fallen across his face, then pulled a scarf from a back pocket and tied it around his forehead. "It'll have to win, right, Vanessa?" Derek seemed as proud of the work as if he had done it himself.

"Thanks." Catty smiled and adjusted the cloth over the canvas.

"We're heading off to the Ramp," Derek announced and put his arms around Tianna. "You guys want to come watch wonder girl ride the fire? She does a monster kickflip."

"Can't today," Vanessa lied and glanced at her watch. "I'm late." She turned and started walking away from them, trying to quell the white-hot jealousy sizzling in her stomach.

"Vanessa!" Catty yelled after her. She caught up to her and smacked the edge of the painting on the ground, blocking Vanessa's path. "I taught you that trick with the watch, and I also know what you were doing at lunchtime when you pretended you didn't have your off-campus pass. What's up?"

"I wasn't pretending," Vanessa said, her eyes daring Catty to challenge her. "I couldn't find my pass, and I have something I have to do now."

She ignored Catty's scowl, stomped around her and immediately felt bad. An urge to apologize overwhelmed her. She didn't care if the truth sounded lame. She'd just tell Catty she was resentful of the way Tianna was crowding into their friendship.

She spun around to apologize, the words already coming from her mouth. "I'm sor—"

But Catty was with Derek and Tianna, animated and talking about the art competition as they walked down the corridor.

Vanessa watched them for a few moments, wishing she had Serena's power to go into Catty's mind and let her know how sorry she felt. She hoped they had been friends long enough for Catty to understand she didn't mean to be acting like queen of the shrews.

She turned to leave and bumped into Michael. He grabbed her to keep her from falling.

The heaviness in her heart vanished as she gazed into his eyes. "I looked all over school for you today." She let her hand slide up his arm. "But I couldn't find you."

"I got here late. You need a ride home?"

"Sure."

They walked arm-in-arm toward the student parking lot, enjoying their closeness.

"So why were you so late today?" she asked.

"Things." He shrugged.

She didn't press him, but wondered if his grandfather had been sick again. Sometimes it took Michael a while to talk about him, especially if he had had to be hospitalized.

The basketball courts were crowded with guys shooting hoops. The coach blew a whistle and they lined up to practice free throws.

Vanessa glanced up at Michael.

"What?" he asked when he caught her looking at him.

She might as well tell him now. The day was already a disaster. It couldn't get any worse. She leaned forward and gave him a quick kiss for courage, but when she started to pull away, he surprised her.

He slipped his hands around her waist and pulled her close to him, pressing his lips against hers in a slow leisurely way that delighted her.

Guys on the basketball court hooted and teased, but she didn't care. She let her arms circle his neck as his hands glided up her back.

"Michael," she whispered, overcome with the intensity of his closeness and the sweet danger in his kiss. Why hadn't he kissed her this way before? The kiss gave her the nerve she needed.

"I know exactly what I want for my birthday." She looked into his eyes. "I've been wanting to ask you this for a while now." She bit her lip and took a deep breath. "Michael, I want to—"

Abruptly he jerked away, his eyes searching behind her, as if something had upset him. Had he seen someone watching them and become embarrassed by their public kiss?

She turned. The whole basketball team had been staring at them, so she couldn't see why he should seem so upset now.

"Maybe we should discuss this another time," he said, pulling her away.

She stared at him. Had he guessed what she was about to ask? But how could he know? Still, she wondered if not letting her ask the question was his way of telling her no. Nothing in the world could be worse!

"Hurry." He took her hand. "We can talk later."

She yanked away and ran to the girls' locker room.

He chased after her, the basketball team hollering words of encouragement.

She hurried inside, the damp smells of mildew, sweat, and wet towels enveloping her as she spread her arms wide.

There was only one way she knew to rid herself of the hurt throbbing through her. Anticipation made her skin feverish. She freed her molecules, her body surrendering the pull of tendons, bone, and muscle. She closed her eyes, enjoying the slow tickling pain of dissolving into a million fragments.

"Vanessa!" Michael yelled and ran into the girl's locker room after her, his boots echoing on the concrete floor.

"You're not allowed in here," she tried to shout at him, but during the transition she rarely controlled her vocal cords. A haunted sound like wind whispering through trees came from her throat.

Michael looked around the room, baffled. What would he do when he found her shimmering like a ghost?

CHAPTER NINE

MICHAEL GLANCED INTO the corner where she stood, but if he saw anything now, it was only a dark flutter between the banks of lockers, before gravity released her and she became no more than a breeze.

She curled around Michael, caressing his face, wishing he had let her speak.

He touched his cheek as though he had felt something more in the air current she had created.

She whisked up, hovering near the ceiling, and looked down at him, still unabashedly standing in the girls' locker room. That wasn't like Michael. Nothing was the same anymore.

"Bye, Michael," she murmured.

A perplexed expression filled Michael's eyes. He frowned and turned. "Vanessa?"

She swirled away and continued outside, the sunshine warming through her, then wove through the rose bushes near the administrative offices, letting the fragrance permeate her cells. At last she leaned back on the wind and soared to the sky.

When she was over Melrose Avenue, she glanced down.

Jimena, Catty, and Serena stood in front of Aardvark's Odd Ark. That's where they shopped for vintage clothes. Vanessa pulled her molecules closer together so that her denser weight stopped her flow, then watched in disbelief as Serena showed off a pink-and-black bowling shirt. Gnawing hurt raced through her. Why hadn't they invited her along?

She watched for a moment, then stretched and swept away, sailing home. She seeped through the crack under her bedroom window and circled her room once to make sure her mother wasn't there before pouring back into her body.

She glanced at her message machine. No flashing light. She couldn't believe Michael hadn't phoned her. He hadn't wanted to listen to what she had to say, and now he wasn't even calling to find out if she was okay or why she had left him so suddenly. If he really liked her, he would have called. The hollow ache inside her grew.

"Mom." She hurried into the hallway, throwing her purse and books on the bed.

She glanced into her Mother's room to see if she were napping, then raced down the stairs, breathing in the sweet smells of fresh baking, and went into the kitchen.

Cookies were spread across the counter, cooling on aluminum foil, the room still holding the heat from the oven. She must have just missed her mother. Some days her mom's schedule made her feel like an orphan. She picked up a cookie and took a huge bite, the chocolate melting on her tongue. Her stomach rumbled in welcome.

She plucked the note her mother had left on her worktable, letting red beads roll into a nest of black, orange, and yellow threads.

Late call tonight. Don't wait up. There's
money for a pizza. I made the cookies special.
Love, Mom

She checked the call sheet tacked on the bulletin board. Tonight they were filming downtown. The crew call was at 3 P.M., the shoot call at 4 P.M. They were doing exterior shots again, but in a safer neighborhood this time. Her mom probably wouldn't be home until early morning.

This had been one of the worst days she could remember. Maybe Michael had never liked her as much as she had liked him. Her stomach clenched at the possibility. That's probably why he hadn't wanted to hear what she had to say. At least she hadn't embarrassed herself by forcing him to listen to her.

For no reason, she thought of Hector. A dreamy smile stretched across her lips as she imagined his hands touching her back. She didn't care if it was make-believe. She wanted to see Hector again. She needed his arms around her, her cheek resting on his chest, the feel of his breath mingling with hers. She wasn't about to stay home and torment herself over the day's events. Her mind made up, she left the kitchen.

Besides, someone needed to investigate. While the others were shopping on Melrose at Aardvark's, Wasteland, and Fred Segal, she might even find Leda and Elena. That's what she told herself, but as she opened the door to the bedroom her mother used for storage, she knew she was making up an excuse in case the others caught her in Hector's arms.

She began rummaging through the dresses hanging on racks, finally pulling out a slinky blue one with long slits up the side and a low-cut back. She hadn't seen it before. She held it up against her chest and studied herself in the mirror. She definitely liked what she saw.

She carried the dress back to her room and flung it onto the bed, determined to ignore her homework and take a nap. She sighed, knowing she couldn't do that. She might need to do something drastic, but that definitely didn't include letting her grades drop. She put her books on the desk, and within a few minutes she was lost in her notes and textbooks.

When twilight had turned to full night, Vanessa put her books aside and dressed. A thrill ran through her as she glanced at her reflection in the mirror. If Hector didn't ask her to dance when he saw her in this outfit, he never would. She twirled again, loving the way the dress exposed her tan legs and back.

When she picked up silver earrings, she saw her left hand. A red serpentine pattern now covered her fingers, and the paisley motif on her palm was complete. Another marking had started growing on her wrist and traveling to the crook of her elbow. She wondered briefly what it meant. She wished the Catty from the future would hurry back and take it away, but for now there was nothing she could do except hide it.

She hurried back to her mother's storeroom, found a pair of elbow-length white gloves, slipped them up her arms, then clasped rhinestone bracelets over her wrists.

At last she went back into her room, stood in front of her open window, and closed her eyes. Her skin began to prickle, and soon undulating vibrations ran through her body. When she became as light as air, she stepped onto the ledge and out into the cool night, drifting higher and higher until she found a current blowing east.

As she neared the convention center, the smells of onions, garlic, and Korean barbecue floated around her. She dove toward the brick apartment buildings, then hiding under a covered porch, she concentrated, forcing her molecules to combine.

She walked down the alley, stepping around people in their makeshift cardboard shelters, and finally hurried up the back steps to Heaven's Ballroom, the music growing louder as she reached the top of the stairs. She pushed inside, took the time card from the manager, and scanned the dancers.

She could feel the eyes of the men looking at her as she walked across the floor. She didn't see Hector, and felt disappointed. She had assumed he would be here. Without him to dance with, she wished she hadn't worn such a provocative dress. She kept her back straight, ignoring the comments from the three men sitting nearby.

"Vanessa." Adriana waved from a red booth. She was wearing a green dress with sequins.

"I'm surprised to see you here," Vanessa said when she joined her. "Does Jimena know?"

"Don't tell her." Adriana brushed a hand through her sleek black hair. "I need the *plata*, just like you do."

Vanessa started to explain that she wasn't here to make money, but stopped. Her real reason sounded worse.

Adriana pushed a wooden bowl of popcorn closer to Vanessa. "It's a slow night." She gazed angrily at the guys sitting across the floor. "I don't know why they come if they're not going to dance. They could buy a beer at the liquor store."

"You hear anything about Leda or Elena?"

Vanessa asked, and scooped up a handful of popcorn.

"*Nada.*" Adriana started to say something more, when a man came over and took her hand. "Got to go." She slung her purse over her shoulder, forcing a smile, then threw her head back and laughed at something the man had said, but when she rested her cheek against his shoulder, her eyebrows crossed in a frown.

Vanessa stood to leave, when someone tapped her shoulder. What was she going to do now? She didn't want to dance with anyone except Hector. Suddenly, she knew she had made one more mistake in a day already filled with too many.

Jimena stood behind her, a curious look in her eyes. "You should have called me," she said. "I would have given you a ride. I didn't know you wanted to come down here to investigate."

"You were busy," Vanessa answered, still feeling angry that they hadn't invited her to go shopping with them earlier today. She glanced at the dance floor. Adriana was pulling the man to the other side of the room before Jimena could see her.

When Vanessa turned back, Jimena was staring at her dress. "Maybe you came down here looking for someone. I warned you this was make-believe."

Vanessa crossed her arms over her chest. "Nobody said it wasn't."

"Have it your way." Jimena shrugged. "I'm glad I found you. It saves me from making a trip."

"Trip?"

"Maggie asked me to get everyone together," Jimena explained. "She needs to see us."

Vanessa shuddered. Maggie only called them together when something bad was happening.

CHAPTER TEN

VANESSA CLIMBED FROM the car and walked up to the entrance of the corner apartment building, a green beach towel, still damp and gritty with sand from Jimena's car, wrapped around her shoulders.

"I still don't understand why you're wearing that dress," Catty repeated for about the fifth time. "It'd be a cool dress to wear to the prom but—"

"I already explained." Vanessa crossed the blue-tiled entry to the security panel and pressed a button marked CRAVEN.

"And elbow-length gloves," Catty continued. "I don't get it."

"Drop it." Vanessa reached for the door handle as a loud hum opened the magnetic lock. She hurried inside, remembering the first night Jimena and Serena had brought her to Maggie's apartment. They had lied to her and told her she was going to meet a retired history teacher named Maggie Craven.

Now she glanced at their reflections in the mirrored entrance. Tianna's knees were bruised; a scrape ran down her arm.

"Did you wipe out at the Ramp?" Vanessa asked.

"Totally." Tianna smiled at Vanessa's reflection. "I rode up the ramp, and when I reached the top, I planted my right hand on the edge and grabbed the board with my left, but I didn't slow the turn enough and fell."

"Too bad," Vanessa said in a sympathizing voice, but secretly she felt something close to glee; perfect Tianna had failed. She glanced up and knew from the half-smile on Serena's face that she had caught Vanessa's thoughts. A blush burned her cheeks.

"Of course, that was the first try," Tianna continued as they crowded into the elevator. "After that, my frontside handplants ripped."

"We'll come down and watch you next time," Serena said and nudged Vanessa teasingly. "Won't we?"

"Great. I love an audience." Tianna checked the bruises on her arm. "It makes me perform better. No chance I'll fall if you're there."

They continued talking about Tianna's athletic ability as they rode the elevator up to the fourth floor.

Vanessa didn't listen. She was thinking about her music. She wished she had Tianna's confidence. That's how she wanted to be about her singing. No rules. Just go where her heart took her.

The elevator doors opened and Vanessa followed the others down a narrow balcony that hung over a courtyard four stories below. She picked at the ivy snarled in the iron railing and watched her friends. The gulf between them seemed to be widening, and she didn't understand why.

On the ride over in the car they had been silent, as if they couldn't think of anything to talk about, and now without her, they were whispering and giggling. Maybe there were only supposed to be four Daughters of the Moon. Could that be why they had been excluding her? Did they know she didn't belong? Worry made her stomach flutter.

Maggie stood at the door, her hair pulled away from her face in a careless French braid. Her head, usually held so proudly, seemed downcast tonight, her shoulders rounded. A dozen necklaces hung around her neck, each bearing an amulet like the one Vanessa wore. When Maggie raised her arms to embrace the girls, the charms hit each other with a musical sound.

Vanessa was the last one to enter. Maggie glanced at her dress after hugging her. "I'm sorry if I interrupted your cotillion."

"My what?" Vanessa asked.

"Never mind. Come in." She sighed and started down the long narrow hallway.

The living room was smoky and smelled of incense. Flames flickered from oil lamps set along the mantel. The fire screen had been pushed back and it appeared that a fire had been burning in the inner hearth.

Vanessa sat down.

The others were nudging each other and staring at the amulets dangling from Maggie's neck, but Vanessa noticed the dark circles under eyes.

"The night before last there was a ring around the moon." Maggie took a deep breath as though she were trying to control a strong emotion. "When the Atrox draws such a ring, it is summoning a powerful demon to earth."

"A demon." Tianna smirked. "I guess he'll be easy to spot."

"Hardly," Maggie cautioned. "When he comes to earth, he assumes a human form and unlike a Regulator he doesn't need to waste his power and energy on camouflaging his real appearance. He becomes flesh and blood like you and me. It will be impossible for you to know him by his appearance."

Serena picked up her amulet. "So we should be watching our moon charms for a warning?"

"Unfortunately, your amulets won't alert you if the demon is near." Maggie continued, the apprehension in her voice growing. "He has the power to control your amulets, and more, I'm afraid."

Catty pulled at a lock of hair, wrapping it around her finger. "But Serena will be able to find him, right?"

"No." Maggie touched the amulets hanging from her neck. "Serena won't be able to read his mind. It is completely impenetrable."

Jimena appeared to be brooding over what Maggie had just said. "Then how do we know when he's around?"

"The only way you'll be able to recognize the demon is by the path of flames he leaves on the ground when he walks."

Jimena sucked in air, looking truly astonished. "*Ya es verdad entonces.* The stories my grandmother and her friends tell about the devil coming to the dance halls and seducing the young girls, they're true."

Maggie nodded. "I'm afraid so. It's extremely important that you never touch the flames he leaves in his footprints."

Vanessa felt a shiver pass through her. "Why not?"

"Because the flame will mark anyone who touches it."

"What does the mark mean?" Vanessa asked, knowing she should show the burn to Maggie, but instead she tugged at her glove, glancing at her arm to make sure the design wasn't showing.

"We won't worry about that unless by some chance it happens." Maggie brushed the question aside. "I need to know why he is here. He's only summoned for something extremely important. Has anything out of the ordinary happened? Anything that might give us a clue as to why the Atrox has called him to earth?"

"My friend Elena disappeared that night,"

Jimena said sadly, and then she told Maggie everything about Elena, Leda, and Heaven's Ballroom.

When she had finished, Serena held up the Devil card from her tarot deck. "After Jimena told us about Elena, I tried to read my tarot cards, but the wind blew them away. All but this one."

"It wasn't any ordinary kind of wind," Tianna added. "It felt alive, like a ghost or something."

Maggie almost smiled. "Yes, that sounds like the demon. He can become invisible like Vanessa, but I'm afraid that he is using Leda and Elena as a lure to trap Jimena."

They stared at Jimena. If she felt any fear she didn't show it. Her face remained hard, her eyes serious.

Secretly, Vanessa felt relieved. If Jimena was the one in jeopardy, then maybe it meant the flame she had picked up in her hallway had nothing to do with the demon and the designs growing on her arm were just more of Catty's pranks. But at the same time guilt tore at her.

How could she feel relieved when one of her friends was in danger?

"Does that mean he's going to turn them to the Atrox if I don't get to them in time?" Jimena asked, showing no concern for her own safety.

Maggie shook her head. "No. He's a demon, not a Follower."

"But if the Atrox can summon him at any time, why did it wait until now?" Vanessa asked, wondering what plan it had for Jimena.

"That's what we need to know," Maggie answered, scowling. "Why now?"

"It doesn't matter why," Tianna said with an easy shrug. "We'll destroy him. How do we beat him?"

Maggie shook her head. "I'm wearing these amulets tonight"—she paused and touched her chest—"to remind myself of how many Daughters I have lost."

Vanessa stared at the charms dangling from Maggie's neck. There had to be ten.

"I can't bear to lose another," Maggie said softly. "If you see the demon, or suspect anyone of being the demon, use any means possible to escape."

"Why?" Jimena looked puzzled.

"Because the demon is perfect," Maggie explained. "There is no way to defeat him."

CHAPTER ELEVEN

ON THE STREET outside Maggie's apartment, Vanessa stared up at the night sky while she waited for her friends to gather around Jimena's car. The clouds appeared to be dissolving as if preparing for the arrival of the moon.

"That was way too spooky," Catty said. "Maggie's never told us there was something that we couldn't beat."

"She looked defeated." Jimena nervously tossed her car keys back and forth from one hand to the other.

"She's keeping something from us." Tianna

opened the rear door. "It was as if she didn't *want* us to beat the demon."

Serena studied the Devil card, then flicked it into the water running down the gutter. It floated away, twirling as it went, before lodging against a discarded water bottle. "Maggie wants to protect the demon until she knows for sure why he's here."

"You read that?" Vanessa asked, smoothing her gloves up to her elbow.

"I felt it," Serena continued. "I had the impression that she was holding something back. Something really important."

"Maggie wouldn't do that. She wouldn't put us in danger," Vanessa argued. "You've become too distrustful since—" She wanted to say "since your breakup with Stanton," but stopped.

"Stanton didn't make me distrustful," Serena countered, as if she had already picked the thought from Vanessa's mind. "When will you stop thinking that I'm still not over him?"

"Sorry." Vanessa shrugged and kept her thoughts guarded. Serena had once cared for Stanton and Vanessa believed she still did.

They had freed him from the Atrox, but afterward he had become a Follower again. Serena felt betrayed by what he had done, even though it had been the only way he could save her from Lambert, a powerful member of the Inner Circle. Now Stanton was Prince of Night, the highest position next to the Atrox. Serena claimed she despised him, but Vanessa had caught her staring into the shadows too many times as if she were hoping to see him.

"Maggie is worried about us," Serena continued finally. "But she's also concerned about the demon."

"I picked that up, too." Tianna looked at Vanessa as if she were daring her to disagree. "Something was definitely up with Maggie. She couldn't hide the way she got all dreamy-eyed when she talked about the demon. I mean, she called the demon 'perfect.'"

Jimena opened the car door. "It's cold out here. Let's go over to Barney's Beanery and get something to eat."

"You go." Vanessa handed back the beach

towel and pulled the gloves above her elbows. She had too much on her mind to go to Barney's. She needed time to think about Michael and her music. "I don't feel up to it. I'll walk home."

"You can't walk down the street looking like that," Catty said.

"Who's going to see?" Vanessa called over her shoulder. "It's not as if I can't disappear."

The roar of mufflers boomed, and Jimena's car screeched away from the curb. Vanessa's stomach knotted. Only a week before, her friends would have forced her to go with them. She stood in the shadows next to a tree and willed her molecules to spread, but they stayed in the comfort of gravity, refusing to move. That happened sometimes when her mood was too down.

She walked passed Cedars-Sinai Hospital, ignoring the stares of nurses and visitors at the front entrance. She continued around the construction site for the new wing of the hospital, then crossed the street to the Beverly Center and started walking toward the Hard Rock Cafe at the corner.

A car pulled alongside her.

"Great," she mumbled, crossing her arms in front of her. She continued walking, eyes straight ahead, ignoring the persistent honking.

Then a familiar voice called her name.

She turned. Hector sat behind the wheel of a red Range Rover, motioning her to join him. His bangs fell in his eyes as he leaned across the seat and opened the car door for her.

She climbed in. "Hey."

"What are you doing walking down the street like that?" he asked, but his eyes told her he liked the way she looked. He studied her for a brief moment before turning out into the heavy traffic on Beverly Boulevard. "I've been driving all over, hoping to find you," he confessed. "I asked some of the girls at the club if you were going to be there tonight. They said you'd left with your friend Jimena."

Vanessa wondered if he had danced with the other women while he had asked his questions. Did he hold them tight in his arms the way he had held her? And then she thought of another question. "How did you know to come all the way over here? It's a long way from downtown."

"I didn't," he admitted. "I'd given up trying to find you. I was just driving home when I saw you." His hand started to touch her thigh, then pulled back. "Seeing you made me think it was destiny."

"Destiny," she whispered with a sigh.

"Yes. I was hoping you'd help me."

"Help you?" That wasn't exactly the destiny she'd been thinking about.

"Adriana told me about Elena and Leda," he confessed. "I need to find them."

"You do?"

He turned down Orlando. When he stopped for the red light on Third Street, he looked at her. "I've been following the demon from Houston."

His words jarred her. How did he know about the demon?

"You can laugh at me if you want." His face remained serious. "But the demon stole my sister." He leaned over and opened the glove compartment. It contained neatly folded newspaper clippings with grainy photos of pretty girls who had disappeared. "I followed him across Texas to El Paso, then on to Phoenix, and finally here. I don't know who this man is, but I'm going to find him. Every day I pray that my sister is still alive."

Vanessa relaxed. He didn't mean a real demon; he meant a man.

She nodded. "I'll help you." It was an easy decision—she wanted to spend more time with him anyway—but then she thought of Michael. Why hadn't he called her?

"Good." Hector patted her hand. The light changed and he turned right, going the wrong way down Third Street.

"Where are you going?" she asked. Her hand clasped the door handle, ready to spring from the car. Had she been careless in trusting a stranger?

CHAPTER TWELVE

HECTOR GLANCED AT her. "Don't be alarmed. There's something we need to do before we go back to the club."

"What?" she asked, as he turned on Doheny and started toward the west side.

"Be patient." His hand patted her exposed thigh. "I'll show you."

Bewildered, she settled back in her seat, but her nerves remained alert, her heart racing.

Less than an hour later he pulled off Pacific Coast Highway near the bluffs in Malibu. Traffic buzzed around them as they climbed from the car.

Vanessa stared out at the phosphorescent waves pounding to shore and breathed the briny smell of ocean and kelp. "I don't understand what we have to do here." She felt cautious, her molecules aroused again, ready to bound free at any moment and float away.

Hector grabbed a bundle of white paper lanterns and a box of wooden matches from the back of the truck. "You'll see. Come on." He started down to the beach.

She kicked off her shoes, threw them onto the seat, slammed the door and walked barefoot over the ice plant, following him to the shoreline.

As the moon rose, he opened one of the lanterns and lit the long cord hanging from its center. He glanced back to Vanessa. "The lanterns will take our prayers to the heavens and show our seriousness in capturing the demon."

"Do you mean a real demon?" Her arms quivered.

"What do you think?" he joked. Then he held the sides of the lantern, his face lit by the fire's glow. The wind lashed the flame at the end of the rope. The heated air made the lantern buoyant. He closed his eyes as if saying a prayer and released it.

Vanessa was awestruck, watching it drift up, an orange glow in the black sky.

Then Hector opened his eyes and lit the cord on Vanessa's lantern. He handed it to her. Her fingers began to tremble when they touched the thin paper. Her head throbbed as she stared at the flame.

Hector stood behind her and wrapped his arms around her. "Clear your mind and let the universe know you are intent on having this demon for your own," he whispered into her ear. "Pray for the universe to grant your desire."

Vanessa closed her eyes, her heart racing, and released the lantern. She opened her eyes and watched. The lantern swayed, then jerked upward as it caught a breeze, but instead of feeling thrilled she felt a sudden sense of doom and wondered why such beauty should fill her with dread.

"Do you want this demon?" Hector asked again, pulling her away from her thoughts.

"Yes," she answered. She didn't think she had ever wanted anything more.

"Then think that as I send the other lanterns into the sky." Hector lit the cord of another lantern and then another until dozens were drifting over the ocean, the flames sparking beneath the orange glow of the paper.

"This is the last one, Vanessa." He lit the cord and handed it to her.

She closed her eyes, prayed silently to capture the demon, and released it. When she opened her eyes again, Hector was standing inches from her face. He paused as if asking permission and when she didn't pull away, he leaned over and kissed her lips.

A tremor of doubt shimmered across her mind as she felt his mouth on hers. How could she do this to Michael?

She pulled back and looked at Hector, his eyes half-closed, and then an insolent smile formed on her lips. She wasn't *doing* anything to Michael. He had had his chance. He could have called her tonight or come over to her house, but he hadn't bothered. Besides, who was going to tell him? And as she leaned in to kiss Hector again, another painful thought came to her. Maybe Michael wouldn't care.

Hector sat down in the sand, pulling her with him. "Let's watch until the lanterns disappear."

She rested her head on his shoulder, listening to the pulsing surf, and watched the last lantern become a red bead in the starry night before it vanished.

"We'd better go." Hector sat up and brushed sand from his slacks. When he did, Vanessa caught a glimpse of something gold reflected in the moonlight.

She reached for his pant leg and pulled it up. It looked like a gold band with an intricate serpentine design etched into the metal. "It's beautiful. Let me see."

Hector jerked his leg away from her.

"What is it?" she asked.

"Ankle bracelets." He stood, took her hand and pulled her up. "They're a custom where I come from."

"Where is that?" she asked, again aware of his accent.

He didn't answer. Something had caught his attention.

She glanced down. Her gloves had fallen below the elbow and he was staring at the filigree pattern etched into her skin.

"It's a henna tattoo," she lied and tried to laugh. "Do you like it?"

"I love it," he said reverently. He removed the rhinestone bracelet and peeled the glove down her arm. A sigh escaped his lips as if he were overcome by the beauty of the design. He turned her hand and ran his fingers lightly over the twisting lines. Under the moonlight the red starburst on the back of her hand radiated like fire.

"This is so lovely," he whispered. "You shouldn't hide it under gloves."

He tossed her gloves in the sand.

CHAPTER THIRTEEN

HECTOR STOPPED AT the back door to Heaven's ballroom. "I'll go in first," he told Vanessa. "So no one will think we're together."

"Okay," she agreed. "But don't forget to ask me to dance. I don't want to get stuck with some guy I don't know."

Hector smiled. "Don't worry so much." The hinges of the door squeaked as he pulled it open and entered.

Vanessa waited, rubbing her arms against the cold, and glanced at the moon peeking over the burned-out apartment building behind her.

She held up her left hand, wondering at the way the design sparkled in the moonlight, then entered the club.

The air inside was sultry now and filled with thick cigar smoke. The dance floor had become a noisy display of twirling bodies and fast-kicking salsa feet. Adriana was dancing with the same wiry man, her smile strained.

"*Hola.* Welcome back." The manager licked his thumb, pulled a time card from the stack clutched in his fingers and handed it to Vanessa.

Immediately, Hector grabbed her around the waist and danced her to the time clock.

"Do you see anyone?" He spoke close to her ear.

"What am I looking for?" she asked. Followers were easy to identify, but she'd never chased a demon before. Maggie had said the demon left a track of flames. She strained to look beneath tapping feet.

Hector laughed. "What do you think you're going to find crawling across the floor? He's not a snake."

She shrugged and snapped her time card into the machine.

After they had danced for a while, Hector pulled away. "I like you, Vanessa." His eyes filled with delight. "Go wait in one of the booths. I'll get us some Cokes."

When he hurried off, Vanessa looked around the room for Adriana. She didn't see her now and wondered if she had gone home. She stepped closer to the back door, hoping the air would be less smoky there. The manager had fallen asleep, his chin resting on his chest.

Vanessa quietly opened the door and froze. A woman's scream filled the air. It was far away and almost hidden by the loud music, but she was positive she hadn't imagined it. She darted back inside, shoved through the dancers and looked for Hector at the canteen. He wasn't there. He must have gone to the rest room. She couldn't wait for him, not if someone were in trouble. She squeezed back through the dance floor and hurried outside, pausing on the landing.

The hum of rooftop air conditioners and

window fans was the only sound she heard now, but as she stepped down the creaking stairs, another scream pierced the night.

She kicked off her shoes and sprinted down the alley, her feet striking stones, oil stains, and scummy rags. She had only gone a short distance when she caught the clatter of someone nearby kicking through bottles and cans. She stopped running and held her breath.

When the noise didn't return, she crept into the dry weeds growing next to a pile of old tires and peered out. Moonlight reflected off the broken glass in the alley. A flickering security lamp in a carport made shadows dance. Three homeless people lay curled in blankets next to a rusted car on cinderblocks. But she saw nothing she could blame for the sense of danger she felt rising inside her.

Footsteps broke the quiet.

She edged into the darkness behind her, the smells of engine oil and gasoline fumes becoming stronger. Her hands touched a rack stacked with rows of hubcaps. She used the edge to guide her as she stepped backward into the work area of a mechanic's garage.

The footfalls seemed closer now.

She took another step into the inky shadows and tripped. As she tumbled backward, she grabbed a shelf, hoping to stop her fall, but the board snapped in two. The silence exploded with the metallic clang of hubcaps hitting the ground, rolling into the alley, and spinning before they finally settled.

Vanessa struggled up, ready to run, her heart beating wildly against her chest. Then her hands touched what she had tripped over. Air hissed through her lips as she clenched her jaw to hold back a scream.

Adriana lay on the ground in front of her.

Vanessa gently shook her. "Adriana," she whispered, desperately trying to rouse her. When she didn't respond, Vanessa pressed her hand under her nose. Warm air caressed the tips of her fingers. At least she was alive.

Another sound made Vanessa alert. The alley echoed with the rap of running footsteps.

Whoever it was would find them in seconds.

Frantic, she looked for a place to hide. She rolled Adriana behind a stack of tires, then crawled beside her. It was the best she could do, but they were too exposed.

Adriana groaned and coughed.

"We need to be quiet," Vanessa cautioned, hoping that some part of Adriana's consciousness would be able to understand their danger.

The steps were slow now and near.

Vanessa peered out between the stacks of tires as a man walked into the garage. Thin threads of smoke curled around his pantlegs, writhing into the air with a sulfurous smell.

She shifted her weight and strained her neck until she could see his shoes. As one foot lifted, black-red flames appeared and twisted across the ground, consuming bits of paper and dried grass. A small fire started in a gasoline stain, but it gave off no light to help her see better.

She tried to catch a glimpse of the demon's face, but from her angle it was impossible to see above his waist. Then a noise farther down the alley made him turn and run before she had a chance to change her position and look again.

Relief flowed through her, and she took in long slow breaths. She placed a hand across Adriana's forehead. Her skin felt cold and wet. She had to take her someplace safe.

She pulled Adriana against her and focused on changing. A barb of pain jolted through her as she tried to release her molecules too quickly. She concentrated on loosening her body gradually. She watched in wonder as Adriana's hands blurred, then stretched, fluttering in the dark before becoming a mist.

Then they were both invisible, lifting over the tires and hubcaps. She decided to take Adriana to Jimena's apartment. Even if Jimena weren't home yet, her grandmother would be and she'd know where Adriana lived. Then again she wondered if she should take her up to County General Hospital.

Before she could decide, she felt Adriana shudder. Her molecules rippled as if the cold were awakening her.

"It's all right, Adriana," Vanessa whispered. "You're with me. Try to relax."

But Adriana wrestled against her hold, trying to break away. Then suddenly Adriana screamed, and Vanessa almost dropped her.

"Be quiet!" Vanessa ordered.

Three homeless men scrambled from their tangle of blankets and rushed into the alley, eyes searching the dark shadows.

Adriana hadn't found her voice yet but she was yelling anyway, the words coming out with eerie, haunting sounds as she struggled to free herself. With each turn her body became denser. Already Vanessa could see one hand clawing at the air.

"You're safe." Vanessa tried to calm her, but Adriana only fought harder, her lashing molecules sending a torrent of pain through Vanessa.

One of the homeless men spied the hand and pointed up. The other two looked up as Adriana's leg appeared in the air above them and kicked.

It was too much weight to stay airborne.

Vanessa and Adriana tumbled to the ground, materializing as they fell. Vanessa plunged into garbage, her dress ripping. Her skirt tore free as they rolled through discarded crating material, Adriana punching and yelling at her.

"¡*Bruja!*" Adriana screamed and sat up, pointing an accusing finger at Vanessa. "You're the Devil's helper!"

The homeless men took careful steps toward them.

Vanessa tried to reason with her. "I saved you from the Devil."

Adriana stood quickly, terror in her eyes, crossed herself, and sprinted away, limping.

Vanessa folded her arms on her knees and rested her head. This was the worst day of her entire life.

Slowly, she stood and started walking. She could go back to Heaven's Ballroom, but she didn't want to do that, given the way she looked now. Part of her dress was missing. She had to become invisible again in order to go home, but she wasn't going to do it in front of an audience.

The three homeless men cast nervous glances at her, stepping back into the shadows.

"I am not the Devil's helper," she mumbled angrily as she walked by them.

She hurried past a rubble-strewn lot filled with clusters of plastic and cardboard huts, then turned onto a side street and almost set her foot in a line of flames twisting across the sidewalk. She jumped back into the alley, her heartbeat thundering in her ears, and pressed against the cold brick wall. She took one sliding step backward and bumped into someone.

CHAPTER FOURTEEN

FEAR PULSED THROUGH her and she struggled against the arms holding her. The person was dragging her back, away from the light.

"Vanessa, what's wrong?"

Her head jerked up. "Michael?" She stopped fighting and turned.

Michael crossed his arms and looked as if he were waiting for an explanation. He wore a black leather motorcycle jacket over tattered jeans and a worn T-shirt. A red scarf swept his hair away from his forehead. This time he was wearing his earring.

"What are you doing here, Michael?" She tried to catch her breath.

"Looking for you."

"Me? Why would you think I'd be down here?" She cast a worried glance over her shoulder, expecting the demon to return.

"I was playing pool at Barney's earlier. Your friends came in, and I asked about you. Jimena told me I'd find you down here." He pulled her under an amber circle of light near a garage and looked down at the torn dress, then worked his thumb over her cheek as if he were cleaning away dirt or worse. "It took me forever to find you," he said at last. "What are you doing down here anyway?"

She grabbed his hand, stepped in front of him, and started walking. "I'll explain, but right now we have to get away from here."

When he didn't follow, she glanced back. He was staring at her backside and he didn't bother to hide the surprise in his eyes.

"Michael!" she scolded as she became aware of how little she was wearing. One panel of her skirt had torn away, exposing her leg and more.

"Why are you dressed like that, Vanessa?" He took off his jacket and handed it to her.

"Thanks." She tied the sleeves around her waist, breathing in the jacket's leather smell. "I'm dressed this way for a reason."

"Obviously." He looked wounded, his lips moving as if he were trying to find the words to express how he was feeling, then his hands fell to his sides. He turned and stomped away.

Vanessa ran after him, pebbles and bottle caps pricking the bottoms of her feet. "I came down here to investigate," she said, hoping he would believe her.

"When Jimena told me you'd probably be at Heaven's Ballroom, I didn't believe her." He quickened his pace. "Do you know what that place is?"

She wondered if Jimena had told him she was dancing for dollars. Then another thought intruded: had Jimena directed him down here, hoping he'd find her dancing with Hector?

"If you'd needed money that badly," Michael

continued angrily, "I would have given it to you without making you dance with me."

"Jimena should have told you why I was down here." Vanessa tried to touch his arm but he jerked it away. "We all came down here yesterday because Jimena's friend Elena had disappeared. Then tonight I thought I heard someone screaming and when I went outside I found Adriana—"

He stopped. "Where is she now?"

"I scared her. She accused me of being a witch and ran away." Even in the dim light she could see from Michael's expression that he wasn't believing her.

"Why can't you just tell me the truth?" Michael turned and hurried away from her.

She ran after him and accidentally stepped on a piece of glass. It sliced into her big toe. "Ouch!" She stood on one foot and tried to pluck out the sliver of glass.

Michael turned, took two steps back to her, then with a quickness and strength that seemed impossible, he swung her into his arms. "How could you do this, Vanessa?"

"I told you," she muttered.

Michael waited until she had picked out the shard, then he pressed her tight against his chest and started walking. She slid her arms around his neck, resting her head on his shoulder.

"How can I protect you if you come down here?" he muttered.

Her head jerked up and she looked at him. "Protect me? I don't need you to protect me. I can take care of myself."

"Right," he smirked. "That's why your dress is torn, your shoes are gone and your face looks like you were crawling through a Dumpster."

They came to the end of the alley. Now they were on a street where homeless people had made makeshift shelters for the night. Michael hurried to a parking lot, empty except for his cousin's car.

He set her down gently, then unlocked the passenger side door and helped her into the seat.

He hurried around to the driver's side, opened the door, and slipped behind the wheel with one easy motion, then slid his arm across the seat and stared at her, his eyes angry. "Don't go down there again. Promise me you won't. It's not safe there, especially for you."

"Michael, didn't you hear me when I told you why I came down here?"

"Stay away." Without another word he stuck the key in the ignition and slammed his foot on the accelerator. The car blasted into the street with a squeal of tires, leaving a cloud of bluish exhaust in its trail.

"It's obvious that you're angry. Can't we discuss this?" And then another worry found her. Could he have seen her with Hector? Maybe he had gone into the club and watched her dancing with Hector, then followed her when she went outside.

Her stomach dropped. Why had she risked everything to be with Hector? She didn't know him the way she knew Michael. She didn't like him as much as she liked Michael, so why had she kissed him? She hated to think she had used Hector because she was feeling low and wanted someone to boost her ego. She had never thought she was that kind of person.

They drove in silence. When the car stopped in front of her house, Michael didn't jump out and open the car door for her.

"I'm sorry, Michael." She had the definite impression that he wanted to kiss her, but when she leaned forward, he tilted his head away and stared out the window.

"Good night, Vanessa."

"Can't we talk about this?"

"I've said everything I need to say."

"Michael, really, I can explain everything that happened. *Everything*."

When he didn't answer, she opened the car door and got out. Immediately, the car swung away from the curb. Music pounded from the inside, shattering the quiet night.

She watched the car speed away, and remained on the curb in the chill air until she could no longer hear the boom of mufflers and music.

"Congratulations," she grumbled, defeated. She had succeeded in doing the impossible; she had made the worst day of her life even more miserable. She glanced down at her big toe. At least it had stopped bleeding and no longer hurt.

She needed to talk to Catty. She hurried inside, glad to be home, flung Michael's jacket on the couch, then ran up the stairs to her bedroom, turned on the light, and caught her reflection in the mirror.

Dust and oil covered her face. The dress was torn and stained. She didn't even want to consider the funny green mess on the bodice. She was never going to be able to explain this to her mother. She slipped out of the dress, wadded it into a ball, and threw it in the trash.

She punched the speed dial button for Catty's number.

Catty's mother's sleepy voice answered.

"I know it's late," Vanessa explained. "But can I talk to Catty?"

"Catty is spending the night with Tianna," she answered. "Do you need her telephone number?"

"No," Vanessa answered and hung up, shocked by the depth of her hurt.

CHAPTER FIFTEEN

VANESSA WOKE EARLY the next morning. The anxiety had been building in her through the night, and now she needed to act. She was going to tell Michael what she wanted for her birthday no matter how embarrassing it became. What did she have to lose? If he laughed at her, so what? It couldn't be any worse than the way things were right now.

She tugged on black slacks, a fuchsia short-sleeved T-shirt, and her Doc Martens, then started to pull on a hooded, zip-front sweat jacket and stopped. She twisted her arm, admiring the arabesque curling across her skin. The rich, curving patterns and flower shapes glimmered in the sunlight falling through her window.

Abruptly, she stuck her arm into the sleeve and pulled the sweat top on. She didn't need any more kids at school asking about her henna tattoo. She dug into her dresser, found a pair of black gloves, then tugged them on as she ran out to the hallway and thundered down the stairs.

Michael's leather jacket was still on the couch where she had tossed it the night before. She grabbed it and hurried outside. She had hoped that Michael would be waiting to give her a ride to school. But when she didn't see his car, her determination strengthened. She took long strides down the sidewalk and couldn't stop grinning as she imagined the surprised look on Michael's face.

When she reached La Brea High, she saw Jimena leaning against the wire-mesh fence, dressed in low-rise jeans that showed off her slender waist. Serena stood beside her in graffiti-covered jeans with side slits up to her knees.

"Vanessa!" They called, waving her over to them.

"Adriana came by last night." Jimena said. She looked as if she was having a hard time holding back laughter. "You really scared her."

"I know." Vanessa pulled her sunglasses up, scanned the school ground for Michael, then looked back at Jimena. "I had to make her invisible. It was the only way I could get her to safety."

"I figured you saved her from the demon." Jimena's smile was huge. "But she thinks you're a *bruja* now. She came pounding on my door late last night and said you made her fly."

"You think she'll tell anyone?" Vanessa asked, wondering why they thought it was so comical.

"She already told everyone she knows." Serena leaned against Jimena, giggling.

"Did they believe her?" Vanessa felt panicked.

"Sure, but I told them you weren't a witch,

but a powerful *curandera*." Jimena paused, then added, "Now all my grandmother's friends will be coming to see you with their bunions and toothaches." Jimena and Serena burst out laughing.

Catty ran up to them, wearing a floaty green sweater and black capris. "What's so funny?"

Tianna joined their circle. "What gives? I could hear you laughing all the way down at the corner."

Vanessa told them about rescuing Adriana the night before, but her thoughts kept jumping to Michael. Where was he? She felt heartsick. She wondered if he had stayed away from school because he was so upset with her.

By the end of the day, she still hadn't seen Michael. But that didn't stop her. She had a clear-cut plan. She was going over to his house. She shut her locker, dodged around the kids gathering for detention, and hiked down the hallway with firm steps.

"Vanessa!" Catty ran up to her, her bag

bouncing against her side. "I won the school-district art contest."

"Congratulations!" Vanessa hugged her.

"Can you come with me?" Catty nervously tugged at the sleeves of her sweater. "I made an appointment to get my nose pierced!"

Vanessa felt as thrilled as Catty looked. "To celebrate winning the contest?"

"That's not big enough," Catty said with excitement growing in her eyes. "It's something more important than that."

"More important?" Vanessa wondered what could be more significant. Catty's artwork was everything to her.

"I know what I'm going to do when I turn seventeen," Catty whispered.

"You mean the transition?" Vanessa asked in hushed tones.

Catty nodded. "Tianna and I decided together last night."

Vanessa felt a pang of jealousy. She couldn't hold back her grievances any longer. "I thought you and I were best friends." The words rushed from her mouth. "We promised we'd make that decision together."

Catty's seemed surprised. "It just happened. I didn't do it on purpose."

"We used to share everything." Vanessa's throat tightened and angry tears pressed to her eyes.

"Share everything? You mean personal stuff, like two-timing Michael?" Catty placed both fists on her hips. "Do you know how much it hurt to hear about it from Jimena? She told me you went down to Heaven's Ballroom looking for Hector. Why didn't you tell me?"

"I wasn't two-timing—" She stopped. "Did Jimena tell everyone?" Maybe that was why Michael hadn't come to school today.

"She's not a gossip. Only the four of us know about Hector, but it's not as if I had to hear it from Jimena. I've got eyes. Last night you wouldn't go to Barney's with us because you were meeting him."

"I was not," Vanessa said, trying to defend herself.

Catty's anger turned up a notch. "Do you really think we wouldn't follow you until you became invisible to make sure you were safe? We saw you get in the car with him. The others thought it was funny, but I felt hurt that you hadn't confided in me."

"There's nothing between Hector and me," Vanessa protested.

"Whatever." Catty turned and started to walk away.

"All right." Vanessa caught up to her. "I'm sorry. I'm just so embarrassed and flustered about the way I feel. I more than like Michael. He's everything to me, but I can't get Hector out of my mind. I want to see him again. How can I like two guys at once?"

Catty smiled. "Same way I can like both you and Tianna. But no matter what, you're still my best friend."

"You really mean that?" Vanessa felt a weight lift from her shoulders.

"Of course."

They started walking toward Melrose Avenue, arm in arm.

By the time they reached Tattoo You, Vanessa and Catty were laughing about their misunderstandings. A sign on the window read WE ALSO PIERCE, BRAND, AND CUT. The smells of alcohol and singed hair greeted them when they opened the door. Vanessa read a plaque hanging on the wall: MEMBERS OF THE ASSOCIATION OF PROFESSIONAL PIERCERS.

"My mom checked it out." Catty rang the bell on the counter. "They use hospital-grade sterilization."

"I don't know." Vanessa glanced at the pictures of their branding and cutting work. "It might be painful."

"Come watch." Catty tugged on Vanessa's arm. "Maybe you'll want one, too."

"No way." Vanessa made a face and sat in a yellow chair.

A man with short-cropped hair stepped through a purple curtain. Three silver barbells pinched the skin over his right eyebrow. He had shaved off the left brow and tattooed a snake in its place. He ran his finger down the appointment book, then looked up with a smile. "Catty?"

"That's me. I've got my permission slip." She dug into her messenger bag and pulled out a consent form and handed it to the technician.

"Okay. Follow me." He held the curtain aside for Catty.

She waved and followed him into the back room.

Vanessa stared out the window at the people strolling down Melrose Avenue and thought of Michael.

Moments later, Catty reappeared. "How do I look?"

Vanessa looked up. Her heart lurched when she saw Catty.

"Oh, no," she said as a strange uneasiness flowed through her.

Catty had taken off her green sweater to reveal an off-the-shoulder T-shirt. With the gold nose ring she was dressed exactly like the Catty who had come back to Vanessa from the future.

CHAPTER SIXTEEN

"WHAT'S WRONG WITH it?" Catty gingerly touched the new piercing.

The technician hurried into the room and studied Catty's nose. "It's perfect," he said defensively and scowled at Vanessa.

"It looks great," Vanessa agreed. "Honest." She picked up her purse, hands trembling, and waited at the door while Catty paid.

"What's up?" Catty asked as they stepped into the crowd of kids shopping in the trendy shops on Melrose Avenue.

"You look exactly the way you did the night you came back from the future to warn me." Vanessa tried to hide her alarm. "Same capris, top, nose ring. Everything, except that you don't have black smears on your face."

Catty didn't seem bothered by what she was saying. "Don't be so nervous. I'm sure my visit from the future was some joke. You know me. I already explained."

"Maybe, but you looked so terrified."

"Of course, I did. That would have been part of the joke. Besides," Catty explained. "You can't stop the future from coming, so worrying about it won't change anything."

"You're right." Vanessa agreed reluctantly.

"So if you want to feel lousy, keep worrying, but if you want to feel good think about—"

"Michael." Vanessa grinned, feeling a tickle of excitement as she remembered her decision.

Catty stopped at the corner near Wound and Wound and studied the sci-fi windup toys in the window. "I'm meeting Tianna. You want to come?" She glanced sideways, waiting for Vanessa's response.

"No, thanks," Vanessa said lightly. "I have things to do."

"So I'll see you tomorrow." Catty started to walk away, then looked back. "Meet me at Starbucks in the morning, usual Saturday time."

"That's a deal." Vanessa waved and headed down a side street.

Michael lived close to the school. Soon she was in his neighborhood of small Spanish-style stucco homes with red-tiled roofs.

She couldn't stop the happy feeling rising inside her as she turned down the brick pathway to Michael's home. Automatic sprinklers watered the front lawn, rainbows hovering in the spray. She took that as a good sign and quickened her pace past a row of wet azaleas to the carved door. She stepped onto the porch, where blue tiles bordered the archway, and a gentle breeze pushed the limbs of climbing plants against her.

Love was making her bold. Without stopping to think, she pushed the doorbell, letting it ring twice, then idly picked a sprig of honey-suckle, sniffed it, and leaned against the door frame, fantasizing about Michael with a growing sense of pleasure.

The door opened.

She turned, smiling. "Michael—" She stuttered and stopped the *I love you* from tumbling through her lips.

Michael's grandfather stood in front of her. He was the same height as Vanessa, but twice as wide, his gray hair thinning and long. The aviator glasses were crooked on his broad nose as if he had been napping and put them on too quickly when the doorbell rang.

"Vanessa! Good to see you." He clasped her hand in both of his, smiling. Every wrinkle seeming to show his joy. Behind him guitar music played from a radio.

"Hi. Can I speak to Michael?"

"Michael's been backpacking in Yosemite all week," his grandfather said. "He won't be back until tomorrow. I'm surprised he didn't tell you."

Vanessa started to say *I just saw him last night,*

but instead nodded, trying to keep the confusion from showing on her face. Michael had talked about the backpacking program, but she had assumed he meant the week following her birthday when he had said *next week*. And he had never called to say good-bye.

"Do you want me to give him a message when he gets home?" his grandfather asked.

"No, just give him his jacket." She tried to hand it over but he didn't take it.

"Michael doesn't have a leather jacket."

Vanessa rolled the jacket into a ball and held it tight against her stomach as she tried to push her trembling lips into a smile. "Tell him I came by."

"Sure."

"Bye, now." She waved and rushed down the walk, her shoes splashing through puddles. She could feel Michael's grandfather watching her. She waited until she heard the door close before she gave into her fear with a shudder.

If the Michael she had been seeing wasn't the real Michael, then who was he? She remembered

Toby, a Regulator. He had had the power to change his looks and make her believe he was a high-school student. He had gained her trust. Now she wondered about this other Michael. Was he a Regulator, too? Or worse? Her breath caught. Maggie had never told them what the demon looked like. Could he transform his appearance when he came to earth so that he looked like Michael?

Her heart pounded as an idea came to her. Stanton might help her. Even though he was now Prince of Night, she was safe with him. When he had trapped her in his childhood memories she had tried to save a younger Stanton from the Atrox. Because of that act of kindness, he could never harm her.

But finding him would be dangerous. She'd have to go to the Dungeon, a club in Hollywood where Followers hung out. She took a deep breath and started heading north toward Sunset Boulevard.

CHAPTER SEVENTEEN

THE SUN WAS SETTING when she reached the Dungeon. The outside looked like any of the two-story duplexes dotting the Hollywood landscape. No sign advertised the club inside. Even the cars parked in the drive and vacant lot next door didn't look out of place. Most kids came here when they didn't want the party to end. The Dungeon opened early in the morning, its black decor and walls creating the fantasy of night continuing twenty-four hours a day inside.

Vanessa moved quickly into the shadows on

the porch, then glanced behind her to make sure no one had seen her. All she had to do was sneak inside and see if Stanton was there. She opened the door, heart racing from the rush of adrenaline, and slipped into the club.

A throbbing techno beat vibrated through her as she edged against the back wall, hiding in the darkness, eyes alert. The smells of sweat, perfume, and an overworked swamp cooler filled the clammy air. Immediately her amulet began to glow. She zipped up her sweat jacket to hide its light, then glanced at the silhouetted figures to her right. They were too busy kissing to notice her.

She moved stealthily to the other side of the door, where the shadows were deeper. A guy and a girl sat on the floor, hands all over each other. She stepped around them, tension rippling through her muscles, and stared at the velvet blackness in the corner niche. The more powerful Followers could dissolve into shadow and stay that way for days. She studied the murkiness for any flutter that might betray a hovering shape changer, before cautiously stepping into the nook.

A fanfare of red, yellow, and blue lasers streaked across the smoky room in time with the music. Behind the crowded dance floor, Followers sat on bar stools, sipping drinks and laughing loudly. She recognized the one with the hoops pierced through his nose and lip. His name was Tymmie. Other Followers lounged in hideaway booths, searching the crush of dancers for prey.

She didn't think anyone had noticed her yet.

"Wrong!" Yvonne answered her thought and flicked on a dim overhead light.

Vanessa turned sharply, her nerves on edge.

"Why are you here?" Yvonne had become Lecta last year, one chosen by the Atrox to receive immortality. Now she had her own league of Followers at Venice Beach. She hooked her thumbs over the thick belt that swung below her hipbones and the silver rhinestones circling her belly button. She had cut her hair into a jagged pixie. Wisps of blond hair hung in her eyes and changed color with the flashing laser light.

"Just checking out the action." Vanessa tried to ignore the Followers at the bar who were turning to look at her, their eyes restless and hungry, but in spite of her effort, the fine hairs on the back of her neck rose and her skin broke out with goose bumps.

"I admired your goodie-girl style once," Yvonne went on. "But you don't look very goddess tonight. What is it with those gloves and that sweat top? It's hot. Maybe there's something you want to hide." She smirked and reached for Vanessa's hand as if her curiosity were more than she could bear.

Vanessa jerked back, her amulet pulsing against her with searing heat. "I'm looking for Stanton," she snapped. "Is he here?"

Yvonne tilted her head and tossed her a wicked smile. "Now I understand," she said sarcastically. "You're wearing gloves so you won't get your hands dirty when you try to destroy him."

Tymmie slid from his stool and raised his hand, signaling the others to stay at the bar, then he pushed through the snarl of fast-moving dancers. He had been apprenticed to Stanton once, but since Stanton had become Prince he had joined a new group of Followers who liked to flaunt their devotion to evil. They used the powers of the Atrox, but also guns, knives, and fists. The last time she had seen Tymmie his hair had been white-blond and moussed into jagged spikes. Since then he had shaved his head and had *Atrox* tattooed on his scalp.

"Hey, Vanessa." Tymmie stepped too close, his breath giving off an unpleasant tobacco odor. "Long time."

"I need to talk to Stanton," Vanessa said with determined bravery.

"Royalty." Tymmie arched an eyebrow. "You don't want to mix it up with peasants anymore? I thought maybe you'd come here to bring me back from the Atrox." He chuckled and let his hand slide up her sleeve.

She brushed his hand away.

"You think Stanton wants to talk to you?" Yvonne asked. "Or maybe you've come to ask him to turn you to the Atrox?"

"Just tell me if he's here." Vanessa glanced back at Yvonne and stopped. Her eyes were focusing on Vanessa's chest. Was the amulet bothering her? She didn't think it could be; she didn't see its reflection in her eyes. Still something was troubling her.

"He's not here." Yvonne turned abruptly, grabbing Tymmie's hand and pulling him to the dance floor. She began to move, slinking close to his body.

Tymmie looked confused until Yvonne said something into his ear, then a huge grin crept over his face. He left Yvonne dancing by herself, and shoved through the dancers to the Followers at the bar. He said something and one by one they turned, staring at Vanessa.

She wondered if they were planning an attack. They slid from their stools and watched her, but she didn't feel their thoughts invade her mind or sense any attempt to hold her gaze with their eyes.

She wasn't going to stay. She stepped over the couple on the floor and was about to push through the door when she caught her reflection in a mirrored panel. The leather jacket fell from her hand, and she didn't bother to pick it up. She saw what Yvonne had been staring at. The design now swept up the left side of her neck, clearly visible. She glanced back, wondering if Yvonne had recognized it. Maybe she understood its meaning.

Come dance with me and I'll tell you. Yvonne's words flashed through her mind.

Vanessa considered going back to her, but then her eyes shifted to the Followers standing near Yvonne now. It was too risky to stay no matter how badly she wanted to know the meaning of the design. She was pondering what to do when she saw Hector, sitting in a far booth with a Follower named Kelly. Her heart sank.

Kelly had probably found him downtown, alone and vulnerable, and lured him here with her irresistible California beach-girl look. Hector seemed to be enjoying the way she touched his arm and rested her cheek on his shoulder, but Vanessa knew she was only waiting for the right moment to cross him over and turn him to the Atrox.

The Followers stared at Vanessa, their eyes like dark stones, then their thoughts began pulsing in her mind, trying to put her in a trance.

Terror seized her. She wanted to bolt out the door and run, but she couldn't leave Hector.

CHAPTER EIGHTEEN

VANESSA UNZIPPED HER jacket and let her amulet swing free. Her footsteps pounded heavily on the floor as she shoved around the Followers and elbowed through the head-banging dancers to where Hector sat with Kelly.

Hector glanced up and waved. "Hi, Vanessa."

He seemed excited to see her and started to slide from the booth, but Kelly drew him back, touching his face as if she were trying to force him to look into her eyes so she could entrance him.

"Hector!" Vanessa yelled, hoping she hadn't

arrived too late. She grabbed his arm, tugging him from the booth. "We have to leave."

"What is it?" He looked baffled, but didn't argue. He seemed to sense her urgency and hurried alongside her.

Followers circled them, their eyes blank and deep. Vanessa steadied herself, waiting for their attack, but before it came the music changed, racing full speed into a gunfire beat. A strobe light flashed, and the dance floor exploded into a maelstrom of whirling, kicking bodies.

Vanessa tightened her grip on Hector's wrist and bulldozed through the tangled slugfest of dancers.

Finally, they rushed outside into the cool night air.

"Why didn't you want to stay and dance?" Hector looked hurt.

"Another time." She seized his hand again and led him out to the sidewalk under the streetlight. She studied his eyes to see if Kelly had crossed him over, but he didn't have the haunted, empty gaze of an Initiate.

"What?" He brushed at his forehead. "Do I have something on my face?"

"No." She tried to smile. "You look great. Where are you parked?"

"Over there." He pointed to a vacant lot filled with wild grass next to a liquor store. His Range Rover was parked in the shadows next to a delivery truck.

"Let's go." But before she took a step, she sensed movement behind her and turned.

Followers were filing from the Dungeon, gathering in clusters and lingering on the porch and steps. She felt a sickening drop in her stomach, knowing she couldn't protect Hector from so many.

She glanced at her amulet, surprised to find it was no longer glowing. It should have been throbbing against her, casting off a rainbow of light. She turned back, wondering why the Followers weren't chasing them. The moon hadn't risen so there was nothing in the night sky to make them cautious. They were spilling out to the sidewalks now like people who had gathered to watch a spectacle. The heavy traffic on Sunset Boulevard slowed, motorists craning their necks to see what was happening.

A hand touched her shoulder. She turned quickly.

Hector smiled at her. "I know where to find Elena and Leda." He pulled car keys from his pocket.

"You do?" she asked as they hurried across the dried grass toward the car.

He nodded. "Kelly told me."

"Didn't you wonder how she knew?" she asked, quickening her step.

"Why?" He shrugged. "The information is all I care about."

She couldn't tell him what had almost happened to him inside the Dungeon. He wouldn't believe her if she did. Kelly had probably told him the truth because she had been confident in crossing him over. Then another thought occurred to her. "I thought the demon destroyed the women he captured. Doesn't it seem odd that he's holding them prisoner?"

Hector looked as if he were losing his patience. "Maybe he's waiting for a phase in the moon or a turn of the tide. How would I know? I'm only grateful they're unharmed. Don't you want to rescue them?"

Her stomach fluttered with uneasiness. She wished the other Daughters were here. "Maybe I should call my friends first."

"We need to free Elena and Leda now." Hector seemed optimistic. "If we wait, it could be too late."

"We'll call the police," she suggested.

"But I want to ask them about my sister. The police won't let me talk to them." He opened the door to the Range Rover and waited for her to get inside. "Hurry. They're being held in the abandoned Corona Hotel downtown."

His excitement was infectious but she held back. "I don't think we should go there right now."

"Why not?" He didn't bother to hide his annoyance with her.

"It could be a trap."

He laughed. "Why would you think that?"

"There's a lot about me you don't know." She cast a quick look behind her, worried some Followers might have crept up on them. "You're just going to have to trust me when I tell you it's too dangerous." What would he say if she did tell him the truth? There was no way he would believe her.

He tried to grab her hand as if he were going to pull her into the vehicle, but she took a quick step back before he could touch her.

"I'll get in the car, but we'll go down to Jan's café first and talk about what we're going to do," she said firmly.

"All right." He tried to smile, but she could see his disappointment.

She started to climb in his car when she sensed someone calling her. She turned, her body thrumming, alert to new danger.

A phantom shadow moved near the delivery truck, the quiet around her filling with a soft hiss. Her hair fluttered as if something had stirred the night, and then a black vapor poured from the air, and Stanton appeared in the thick darkness before her.

You were looking for me? The words whispered across her mind.

She could feel his aura of danger as he walked toward her, a sensual smile forming on his lips. He was even more handsome than she remembered, dressed in black jeans and T-shirt, his shaggy blond bangs hanging in his blue eyes. She tried not to stare, but it was hard not to, and then she remembered Hector. She spun around, expecting to see terror on his face, but he was rushing to the driver's side of the vehicle and apparently hadn't noticed Stanton's ghostly arrival.

She stepped closer to Stanton so Hector couldn't hear their conversation. "Do you know anything about someone pretending to be Michael?"

Stanton paused and considered, his eyes unblinking, but he didn't say anything.

"My Michael is out of town, but I've been seeing someone who looks exactly like him," Vanessa explained.

Stanton's eyebrows pinched with sudden anger. "Did he hurt you?"

"No, I just want to find out if there's a Regulator disguised as Michael, and why."

"I sent him to protect you," Stanton said simply.

"You?"

Stanton nodded. "I told him everything I knew about you and Michael so his charade would convince you."

"Why would you send someone to protect me?" Vanessa asked, baffled.

"You were in danger."

She knew in an instant that Serena was the one he had been trying to protect. If one Daughter was at risk, then all of them were in jeopardy. Stanton might be pure evil, but his love for Serena hadn't been destroyed when he had returned to the Atrox.

She could feel Stanton reading her mind. He placed a finger over her lips as if to warn her not to share her thoughts with Serena.

"You once tried to save me from my fate," he

began slowly, his words silky and hypnotizing. "Even though you failed, I remember your bravery, so when I heard that the demon had been summoned to lure you to the dark side, I tricked a Regulator named Finis into helping me."

Stanton eased closer to her, his thoughts touching her gently, searching for a memory of Serena, then he smiled and continued. "The Atrox doesn't use Finis anymore, so he was happy for the assignment. I told him to disguise himself as Michael and watch over you because I wanted to claim you and not let the demon have the glory of seducing a Daughter."

When he spoke again she wasn't sure if his words were coming from his mouth, floating across her mind, or both. "But you're very beautiful, and Finis enjoyed kissing you too much, so after his first encounter with you I warned him that if he kissed you again, I'd make him an outcast."

Vanessa nodded. That at least explained why the other Michael had acted so strangely after their kiss, but even Stanton's warning hadn't stopped him from kissing her a second time. No wonder his behavior had seemed so distant the third time they had met. Then another thought came to her. What would have happened if she had told *that* Michael what she wanted for her birthday? She shuddered imagining how embarrassing that could have been, then she glanced quickly at Stanton, hoping he hadn't read her thought.

A devious smile crossed his face, and she knew in an instant that he had been in her mind. The heat of a blush rose to her cheeks.

Stanton looked over her head, his eyes glinting yellow. "I'm sorry, Vanessa."

"Why?" she asked. "Michael—I mean Finis—did a good job. He's rescued me twice."

Stanton nodded and looked back at her. "Finis did his job. I failed."

"You?"

He brushed back her hair, his finger tracing over the design on her neck. "I didn't protect you. The demon has already marked you."

She caught a flash of remorse in his eyes.

"Hector has succeeded," Stanton whispered. "I'm sorry."

"What do you mean 'Hector'?" Her head whipped around and she gazed at Hector. The truth hit her. When she turned back, Stanton was already dissolving into shadow.

There's nothing I can do to help you now. The words flowed through her with an icy chill.

She spun around again.

Hector was walking toward her, no longer bothering to hide what he was. Red flames ignited beneath his shoes, scorching the dirt and burning the dried grass, but the fires gave off no light.

CHAPTER NINETEEN

VANESSA TRIED TO RELEASE her body and turn invisible, but every time her molecules gyrated out, they struck a barrier and fell back. Air squeezed around her with a python's strength, clamping tighter until her lungs labored to draw in a breath. Intuitively, she knew Hector was restraining her.

He walked toward her with slow easy steps, thin tendrils of smoke wreathing behind him.

Followers pushed into the vacant lot, restless

now, whistling and jeering loudly. Vanessa suddenly understood that she was the show they had been waiting to see.

"You never lost a sister," she said, stalling for time to clear her mind. "That was a lie to gain my trust."

He nodded.

"And you were never trying to find Elena and Leda." Her voice strained against his force.

"Of course not." He stopped in front of her. "I'm holding them captive. A lure to draw you to me if other things failed. I knew you wouldn't stop until they were freed." He tried to take her hand, but she jerked it back.

At once, the pressure tightened around her, becoming unbearable. She rubbed at the crushing weight on her chest, trying to ease the pain.

His hand shot out again and grabbed her wrist. When she didn't fight him, the heaviness of the air seemed to lessen.

He peeled off her glove, his eyes delighting in the glimmering lines of the arabesques on her skin. He gently pulled her sweat jacket from her shoulders, then slipped it down her arms, letting it fall to the ground.

"Why didn't you just destroy me?" she asked. "You had the opportunity."

"Why would I destroy something I cherish?" His fingers lovingly traced over a curving line scarred into her skin.

She glanced at him, wondering if he truly cared for her. His eyes looked sincere, even tender.

"Your sixteenth birthday is only a few days away, and you need to know the truth before then." His arms slipped around her.

"Truth?" Vanessa asked, feeling a sense of foreboding.

"Maggie has convinced you that you're a Daughter of the Moon." He studied her, looking for a reaction. "But you're really a Daughter of Pandora, not Selene."

"That's not true," she protested. She didn't want to believe him, but already a tremor of doubt was creeping into her mind. Could that have been why she had tried so hard to be perfect? Not breaking any rules, always being nice, knowing deep down she had something terrible she needed to hide.

"You've been dreading the approach of your sixteenth birthday," he said as if he had sensed her uncertainty. "Because you've always felt that on that day you would discover your true inner self."

Vanessa suddenly understood her turmoil. It had never been about facing the transition on her seventeenth birthday. She didn't need the courage to choose then; it was *now* that she needed courage.

"Do you remember how hard it was for Maggie to convince you that you were a goddess?" he asked, as if he shared her memories.

She nodded, suddenly eager to hear what he would tell her. The squeezing force eased as she gazed into his eyes. "Why couldn't I believe her?"

"Because part of you had an allegiance to the dark already," he replied.

"No!" she tried to shout, but the word didn't come out forcefully. It was weak and unsure. She cast her eyes away from him.

"Why was the Atrox able to enter your dreams and not the dreams of the other

Daughters?" He touched her chin and made her look at him.

Vanessa shook her head. "I don't know," she whispered. Serena, Jimena, and Catty hadn't been plagued with the nightmares that had tormented her.

"Your unconscious mind had invited the Atrox to merge with you." He pulled her to him.

"That can't be true," Vanessa said, but her confidence was wavering.

"That same part of you is demanding expression now. Let me help you." He leaned forward and tried to kiss her.

The touch of his lips repulsed her now. She wrenched back, rejecting him. In the same moment, the air crushed painfully around her, strangling her.

"You've been fighting your darker self for too long," he explained, smiling at her struggle. "That's why you've felt as if you don't even know who you are anymore. You've been letting too many people define you, because you're terrified by what you sense living inside you."

She stopped fighting, remembering how she had felt a need to do something drastic before she lost herself completely. She had never thought it could be something as earth-shattering as this. She didn't want to listen to him, but she couldn't bring herself to pull away. What he was saying felt right.

"You have all the gifts that were bestowed upon Pandora," Hector continued. "Beauty, talent, and even the wickedness that Hermes put in her heart. Let your darker spirit live."

"No," Vanessa whispered and fought back the hot tears pressing into her eyes. "I'm a Daughter of the Moon, a force of good."

Hector gently lifted her hand and held it up so she could see the design engraved in her skin.

"If Pandora's spirit weren't alive inside you, the burn from my flame couldn't have flourished into such beauty. It would have blistered and tormented you."

She looked at the ornate entwining peacocks.

"You like the peacocks?" He didn't wait for her answer. "Their feathers are a symbol of love and desire."

She glanced at the waves circling her wrist.

"Yes, look at the waves, Vanessa. They denote passion and longing. The design can only express what is inside you. You want something more in your life. Your heart is filled with passion that you have been unable to express. Why deny your true self any longer? Like Pandora, you were born to spread sorrow. Can you continue to deny that part of yourself?"

She shook her head, resigned to her fate.

"It's time to allow your deeper self to be expressed." He looked into her eyes again with an affection that seemed sincere. "Then you'll feel your true power."

Hector studied her, then bent forward to kiss her. Her body revolted against his touch, but she was afraid of having the oppressive force field return. She surrendered, gliding her arms around his waist and up his back, imagining he was Michael, and returning his kiss as passionately as she knew how.

Immediately, the strange imprisoning feel of the air vanished.

She breathed freely, then yanked back, spitting at him in disgust.

"This is my true power!" she yelled and burst into fragments, her molecules expanding outward.

Pain seared through her as muscle, bone, and blood tore apart and swirled into the night sky.

CHAPTER TWENTY

VANESSA WHIPPED INTO the night air, skimming around the numerous billboards on Sunset Boulevard that advertised the latest movies. Instinct told her that even though she was invisible, Hector could sense her presence and was following swiftly. She dove low into the buzzing traffic, exhaust and gasoline fumes suffocating her, then darted in front of a Jaguar, before whisking under a Corvette. She stayed there until the heat from its rumbling motor became unbearable.

At last she left the street and rocketed over the House of Blues, the music from inside still trembling through her as she swept down the hill. She rushed past Cedars-Sinai Medical Center, stretching her molecules, then swept over Robertson Boulevard.

Finally, she sped up to the balcony of Maggie's apartment and filtered through the crack in the sliding glass door, materializing in the living room. She coughed, trying to rid herself of the fumes from the cars and trucks.

Maggie sat in front of the fireplace, deep in thought, holding a cup of tea. "I had hoped you would come to me once you learned the truth."

"You knew." Vanessa felt her heart sink.

Maggie nodded. "The way you were hiding your hand. You kept tugging at the glove as if you were afraid it might slip down. So I misled you by saying the demon was using Leda and Elena to lure Jimena to him. Then you became careless, and I saw the mark."

She set her cup on a table next to her, then examined Vanessa's arm, her eyes seeming to read the meaning in the designs. She lingered on the entwining peacocks, then patted Vanessa's hand before releasing her.

"He told me the designs reflected the feelings inside me." Vanessa sat next to the fire to warm the coldness inside her.

"Ones even hidden from yourself." Maggie looked up, her eyes reflecting the red embers. "His mark is almost complete. All that remains for Hector to do now is the ceremony with the lanterns and you'll be bound to him for eternity."

Vanessa felt a jolt of terror as she remembered the night on the beach. "I've already sealed my fate." Then another thought came to her. "You knew his name and you didn't tell us."

A log rolled off the fire and sparks flew into the air, followed by a sinuous trail of smoke.

Maggie stared at it for a moment, then spoke. "I didn't think he'd use his real name." She poured Vanessa a cup of tea, the sweet scent of mint filling the air. She handed it to her, then refilled her own and sat back in the chair, staring at the flames. "Hector was my lover."

Vanessa tried to hide her shock, but a soft gasp escaped her lips.

Maggie smiled. "He wanted to marry me, but I had already gone to the temple of Selene and pledged my life to fighting the Atrox. I was only free to marry if the Atrox were destroyed."

She added sugar to her tea and stirred, the spoon clicking on the side of the cup as she spoke. "So Hector set out to destroy it. I begged him not to go, but his love for me made him fearless."

"He was good once?" Vanessa asked.

"Yes, a brave soldier. But the evil he had set out to destroy consumed him," Maggie explained. "Pride overwhelmed him, making him believe he had defeated the Atrox. So when it offered him the gold bands he thought it was his due, a tribute from the vanquished." She stopped as if the memory had become too painful to remember and sipped her tea.

When she started again, her words were filled with bitterness. "Hector placed the bands around his ankles, anxious to return home and show me. Only then did he realize they were shackles binding him to evil forever. He was transformed into a demon and cast out from Earth."

Maggie looked down, her eyes disturbed. "I wanted to see Hector one last time, but he could only return to earth if summoned by the overlord of the demons."

"The Atrox?" Vanessa asked.

Maggie nodded. "Only the Atrox can open that gate between the universe and Earth."

"The ring around the moon," Vanessa added softly.

"When Hector passes through it, he assumes the appearance he had in his youth," Maggie said.

Vanessa thought of the first time she had seen Hector. He had looked so ruggedly handsome with his sharp, square jaw, dark skin, and curly hair.

"He was beautiful then." Maggie sighed. "And when I lost him I was enraged. I cried, but tears were not enough. I ran to the temple dedicated to Selene."

Vanessa imagined Maggie rushing up the marble stairs, entering a colonnaded temple and throwing herself on the ground in front of a giant ivory-and-gold statue of Selene. She glanced back at Maggie, knowing she had put the image into her mind, but if it was correct, then it meant Maggie had lived for centuries. She stared at her with new wonder.

"I wanted revenge," Maggie continued. "The Atrox had robbed me of my life. My soul was torn in two. Hector had the other half. I pleaded with the Goddess Selene to let me live to see the Atrox destroyed. I vowed to forgo the rest of death until that day, but before she could answer my prayers, the Atrox granted my wish."

"The Atrox?" Vanessa was stunned. "Why would it want to help you?"

"It didn't help me." Maggie frowned, her eyes seeming suddenly sunken and old. "I had failed to ask for perpetual youth, so granting my wish condemned me to age forever. The Atrox has done this to others, but Selene took pity on me and gave me an elixir to counteract the aging."

Vanessa remembered the first time she had watched Maggie drink a cup of tea. The wrinkles around her eyes had vanished, and she had continued to look younger, her hands becoming those of a girl. She had pulled the pins from her bun, and luxurious curls had fallen to her shoulders, her hair no longer gray, but the silky pale blond of shimmering moonbeams.

Maggie seemed to understand what she was thinking. "You watched me transform that first night, but you thought some drug in your tea was making you imagine the change."

Vanessa nodded, awestruck.

"I have guided and loved many Daughters," Maggie continued with despair. "But I have also watched too many die and turn to the Atrox. My relationship with them is short-lived. I must always say good-bye on their seventeenth birthday. And now I am forced to endure Hector's return to Earth without being able to see him or hold him because he is my enemy."

Vanessa could see from the sorrow on Maggie's face that her pain was still intense.

After a moment Vanessa spoke, "But why did he come for me and not the others?"

Maggie glanced at her, the misery still showing in her eyes. "I'm not certain, but . . ."

From the solemn tone in Maggie's words, Vanessa knew she didn't want to hear what was coming next.

"Of all the Daughters you are the only one who denies and hides her dark side."

"Me?" Vanessa asked. So Maggie had watched her struggle.

"You push back your negative emotions, because you're afraid people won't like you. Now what you call your bad emotions are becoming stronger, trying to express themselves. If I have sensed this conflict inside you, then the Atrox has also. It knows it can take advantage of this, hoping to convince you that you are an evil Daughter of Pandora."

Vanessa leaned forward, wondering if this explained the resentment, jealousy, and anger that were becoming stronger than her ability to hold them back.

"When you accept this other part of yourself and allow it proper expression, it will no longer terrify you the way it does now." Maggie touched her cheek. "It will only make you stronger."

Vanessa wondered how she was supposed to express her evil side and still remain a force of good, but right now she had a more immediate problem. She set her tea aside and held up her hand. "How can I get rid of this?"

"You've been marked," Maggie said. "The lantern ceremony is complete. Hector should have destroyed you already. I don't understand why he hasn't. His job is complete, unless . . ."

"Unless what?" Vanessa asked, feeling a tremor of hope.

"Perhaps he saw you as a chance to gain his freedom," Maggie suggested, her eyes seeming to calculate the possibility.

"He thought I could free him?" Vanessa felt shocked. "How?"

"The shackles show his enslavement to the Atrox," Maggie said. "He can't even die unless the shackles are removed, and the only way the shackles will fall away is if a Daughter willingly agrees to wear them. Maybe he had hoped that if he could win your love, you would make the ultimate sacrifice for him."

"What does it mean if a Daughter wears the shackles?" Vanessa asked.

Maggie's face filled with a mixture of surprise and terror. "You can't even consider it. It would mean you were worse than a servant of the Atrox."

"But if Hector were free, he'd no longer be a demon. Then what would happen to his mark?" Vanessa's heart raced as she saw a possibility.

"The mark would disappear, of course, and the lantern ceremony would be meaningless, but there is no way you can release him without becoming enslaved yourself."

"But I don't have a choice," Vanessa argued. "The only chance I have to free myself, is to free Hector. It's my only hope."

Maggie shook her head. "We need to find another way."

"I have a plan," Vanessa said.

CHAPTER TWENTY-ONE

WHEN VANESSA HAD finished explaining her plan, Maggie looked dispirited. She spoke bluntly. "There are too many problems with your scheme."

That wasn't the answer Vanessa had expected. She was sure her idea could work. "Is there something more I should consider?"

"First, you'll need to become invisible faster than you have ever done and flee quickly."

"I've already escaped Hector once," Vanessa argued.

Maggie stood and began pacing. "I'm talking about a speed that in itself could kill you. The shackles will have the power of the Atrox. Do you really think you can do it?"

"I don't know," Vanessa answered. "Do you see any other way?"

"And then you mustn't let him know you are coming. You have to surprise him so you can ask for the shackles before he has a chance to work a force field around you. You won't be able to become invisible if he does and—" Maggie stopped abruptly.

"What?" Vanessa asked, new worry rushing through her.

"You ran from him once. He won't permit it a second time. If he knows you are there, he'll destroy you."

"But I thought he wanted me to free him." Vanessa stood now, confronting Maggie.

"We're assuming that's why he hasn't destroyed you before now, but we don't know, so you must be prepared. Free him even if it is now against his will and flee," Maggie said, but her eyes looked doubtful.

"I can do it," Vanessa insisted stubbornly, not sure if she was trying to convince herself or Maggie. "How will I find him?"

"He told you that Elena and Leda were being held at the Corona Hotel, so I'm confident he'll be waiting for you there."

Vanessa felt ready and started to turn invisible, her hands becoming a gauzy silhouette.

"Wait." Maggie stopped her. "First you must be purified."

Vanessa paused, then reappeared fully. "You mean like a sacrament before dying?" she asked.

Maggie didn't answer, but turned abruptly. "Come with me." She hurried from the apartment.

Vanessa followed up the fire stairs, her body restless, the need to act pressing her to leave.

When they stepped out onto the tarred rooftop, Vanessa was astonished, sensing she had been transported to a sacred place. Normally the glow of city lights reflected off the clouds, hiding the stars, but tonight a million lights twinkled in the clear black sky. The wind caressed her face as if a hand were turning her in the direction of the rising moon, huge on the horizon, peeking over the top of Cedars-Sinai.

Maggie took a piece of blue chalk from her pocket and started drawing a huge grid of dots on the black surface. Her hair curled around her body, her long white gown flapping against her legs.

Once Vanessa tried to speak, but Maggie held up her hand. "Concentrate on the task ahead."

Vanessa became silent, her thoughts turning inward, moonlight soothing her.

When Maggie finished, she handed the chalk to Vanessa. "Connect the dots in fluid lines."

Vanessa stared at the network of points. "That will take hours to do, and I feel ready now."

Maggie forced the chalk into her hand. "It must be done to clear your mind so you won't be susceptible to Hector's seductions."

Vanessa stepped to the middle of the grid, leaned over and drew a curving line. As she worked, her confidence rose and a calm settled in her.

When she had finished, she stood back, admiring the interconnecting lines. It reminded her of the patterns on her hand and arm.

Maggie handed her a small terra-cotta oil-burning lamp. A match flared and Maggie lit the wick, the flame fluttering in the breeze. "Place a lamp on each leaf of the design."

The still night filled with the tap and clatter of lamps as Vanessa set them on the roof.

When their work was complete, Vanessa stepped back, spellbound by the delicate floral pattern burning brightly in front of her.

Maggie touched Vanessa on the chest. "Look and see."

Vanessa tugged on her T-shirt, pulling it down until she saw the tattoo over her heart, its design matching the one she had just created.

"It has magical powers to protect you," Maggie said, picking up a small brass plate with incense burning in its center. The smell of camphor filled the air between them.

"Put your finger through the flame and touch the white ash," she instructed.

Vanessa hesitated.

"The fire represents the brilliant presence of Good in the universe," Maggie encouraged. "Its ash purifies."

"So I am going to my end." Vanessa pressed her fingers through the flame and thought of her mother.

Then Maggie did the same, but when she brought her finger back, she marked Vanessa's forehead. It felt as if she had drawn a crescent moon with the ash.

"Is that also to purify me?" Vanessa asked.

Maggie shook her head. "That is my mark." She spoke the words with a peculiar tension and then she explained, "I want Hector to know that I am the one who has sent you to free him."

Vanessa nodded. "You must have loved him very much."

"Once," Maggie agreed. "Go now."

Vanessa walked to the edge of the apartment building. When she turned to wave good-bye,

Maggie was gone. Only the fires remained, twisting against the wind.

On impulse Vanessa ran back, picked up the brass plate, blew out the fire, and when the ash was cool enough, she slid it into the pockets of her slacks. Then she stepped to the edge of the roof and let her molecules expand slowly, enjoying the luxurious feel of moonlight flowing through her. At once she spread into the cool air until she was no more than a dust of diamonds.

CHAPTER TWENTY-TWO

VANESSA RACED OVER strip malls and traffic, speeding through concrete underpasses until she found Rose Avenue, closed to traffic now. She glided past trucks containing camera equipment and floodlights, then followed the coils of thick rubber cables to the whirring generators that provided electricity for the set. The wardrobe trailer was nearby. She seeped inside through a screen covering a small window.

In the back, her mother sat at a table,

hemming a green skirt. Vanessa rode the breeze of an oscillating fan to her.

"Good-bye," she whispered, the sound no more than a breath of wind. She didn't know if she would survive the next hour, but she couldn't face Hector without seeing her mother one last time.

As if sensing her presence, her mother looked up, fingers trembling, and pricked her thumb with the needle. A drop of blood fell on the white tabletop.

Vanessa stopped herself from comforting her mother. She flowed back into the night.

She soared downtown, circling office towers and skyscrapers going south toward the blocks of red-brick apartment buildings. At last she found the Corona Hotel. Once elegant, the old Art Deco building was now empty and boarded up.

Her molecules clustered, spiraling down like a million dancing fireflies to the trash-strewn alley behind the hotel. She trickled under a large metal door that had been a delivery entrance and materialized inside.

She hadn't been prepared for the endless darkness surrounding her now. She eased forward until she found a wall, then using her hand as a guide, she advanced, her fingers brushing over broken plaster and gluey cobwebs.

When her eyes adjusted to the dark, she stopped. The floor seemed to be moving, circling about her. With a start she realized rats were scuttling around her shoes. She stomped her foot and the squealing rodents raced away.

In minutes her fingers touched a doorjamb. She found the metal handle and pulled, hinges grinding as she opened the door. She stepped into the vaulted entrance of the hotel lobby, then waited, trying to calm her thrumming nerves and catch her breath.

Streetlights shone through cracks in the boarded windows. The room smelled musty. Rain water had leaked inside, staining the fluting around the windows a gray-brown. A mahogany staircase, with zigzag patterns in the wood, led to the second floor. Leda and Elena must be up there. She wondered if Hector were with them.

She crossed the floor and hesitated at the bottom of the stairs, listening, then stepped forward, the wood creaking beneath her feet. She gripped the banister, thought better of it, and moved back, steadying herself against the dusty wall.

Instinct told her that Hector was nearby. The air felt heavy with his presence. The silence gathered around her as an odd tension tightened her chest and made it difficult to breathe. She continued, more quiet than before.

Halfway up, she heard the soft rasp of a door opening. Stealthy footsteps on the floorboards followed. She paused, her heart racing painfully, and stared at the landing in front of her.

Something moved in the corner of her eye. She turned. A fragment of raven-black darkness swam over shadows near the reception desk below. She wondered if shape-changing Followers were gathering to witness her death. And then an optimistic thought came to her. Maybe Stanton hadn't abandoned her after all.

"Stanton," she whispered, straining to see into the murkiness.

The black form stretched up the wall, then slithered through a crack in the boarded window, deserting her. Her shoulders slumped.

She turned back and started up the stairs again.

Two steps more and soft air circled her, nuzzling around her body. She felt, more than heard, Hector whispering for her to turn. She jerked back, banging her head hard against the wall with a loud thump.

Hector stood beside her, his face in a shard of light falling through a crack in the boarded window, his eyes alive with red and orange flames from some internal burning. She knew at once that he must have sensed her presence and become invisible, stealing up behind her before becoming solid again.

A slow smile crossed his face, his fingers brushing at the crescent moon on her forehead. He started to speak, but before he could, she did.

"I've come to free you," she said, staring into

his fiery eyes. "I'll wear the gold bands that circle your ankles."

Immediately the shackles fell from Hector's legs, clanging against each other. He bent to pick them up.

"Don't," she yelled, afraid they would reattach themselves to him.

He knelt on the stairs, before her.

She knew she shouldn't hesitate. She didn't have the time, but this wasn't the reaction she had anticipated, and it slowed her reaction. She had assumed the bands would fly from his ankles to hers, but instead Hector held them in his hands, then placed them on the step beside her. She could feel him lifting the leg of her slacks, and rolling down her sock. She had to leave, but something was dreadfully wrong. Why was Hector staying? He should be rejoicing in his new freedom, shouldn't he? But he seemed to be bowing reverentially before her.

She heard the clank of metal and knew she only had seconds to act. She yanked her foot away, and pounded up the steps. At the landing, she turned back. Hector was staring at her, his eyes no longer glowing with the internal blaze.

"Vanessa!" he called, looking confused.

She took a tentative step back to help him, but then the shackles rolled toward her. She watched in disbelief as they began clanking up the stairs.

She glanced back at Hector. He seemed so helpless and lost, but she couldn't stay to help him. The gold bands were near and spinning toward her.

"You're free now," she shouted.

A roar filled her ears as her body exploded into particles. Pain ripped through her. She blasted out a broken window, the friction with the air heating her molecules as she continued over abandoned warehouses, traversing rooftops and streets, the speed so exhilarating she almost forgot the danger.

Ten minutes later when she neared the San Diego Freeway, she slowed and turned down Westwood Boulevard, flying over cafés, music stores, and boutiques. The marquees on the movie theaters were dark now. Only the homeless claimed the streets.

She continued like a ruffle in the breeze to the UCLA campus. It was deserted except for janitors and campus police. She let her molecules glide down to the grass under the shadows of the large trees near the archways and bell towers of Royce Hall.

Speck by speck she became whole again, free and safe. She couldn't wait to tell Maggie that she had freed Hector.

She started to walk back to Westwood, when she felt an odd weight. She glanced down and screamed.

The gold bands encircled her wrists.

CHAPTER TWENTY-THREE

AN OPPRESSIVE DREAD settled over Vanessa. She yanked at the shackles, wondering if Maggie had betrayed her. Did she know the bands would follow and capture her? She struggled against the metal rings clasping her wrists. Each time she pulled at them, they clamped tighter.

If Maggie still loved Hector, it was possible that she had used Vanessa to free him. That didn't sound like Maggie, but as soon as Vanessa got rid of these gold fetters, she was going to go over to Maggie's apartment and confront her.

She sat down next to the Quad in front of Royce Hall, then swung her arms up and down, striking the shackles against the edge, whacking again and again, until sparks flew and concrete chipped. The metallic echo was still booming when she stopped. Her skin was raw and drops of blood had fallen on the pavement.

She stood quickly, stepped from the shadows of the tree, and looked up at the moon. *"O Mater Luna, Regina nocis, adiuvo me nunc."* But the words that had once soothed her and given her strength now burned her throat. The pale lunar glow felt as if it were setting her on fire. She collapsed on the grass back under the tree. She didn't feel evil. She felt the same as she always had; overly nice Vanessa Cleveland.

An unnatural stillness filled the air, yet leaves in the nearby trees rustled. She knew she was no longer alone. She stood and started to run but stopped. What could a Follower do to her now?

She had nothing to fear. She had already lost everything.

A cloudy form settled beneath the branches, and Hector became visible, stepping toward her. He looked as he had that first night when she had met him at Heaven's Ballroom, his intense dark eyes again kind and captivating.

"Why did you run from me?" he asked, helping her to stand. "I thought you had come to join me."

"I tried to save you, to save us both." She blinked back the hot tears pressing into her eyes. "At least you're free now. Go to Maggie."

He took her hands and examined the wounds on her wrists, then pulled her to him, wrapping his arm around her as if he were trying to comfort her.

She pulled back. "Don't you understand. You're free now. You should be happy."

His stillness made her uneasy, and then he brushed a hand through her hair and cupped her cheek. "I never needed to be freed, Vanessa. I thought your act was one of love."

A chill ran through her. Now she understood why he had bowed before her to clasp the shackles around her ankles. He thought he had won her affection.

"I was once cast out from Earth," he explained, "and sentenced to live as a demon against my will, but that was centuries ago. The shackles don't enslave me. Now I wear the gold bands as a symbol of my devotion to the Atrox."

Vanessa shook her head in disbelief. "But, Maggie—"

"Maggie doesn't know. How could she? She remembers me as a soldier boy who fell in love with her. She doesn't understand what I've become. You'll understand when you are my bride."

"No," Vanessa whimpered.

"You'll become as dedicated to the Atrox as I am."

"Never!" she cried.

He pointed to the sky. "As soon as the ring surrounds the moon, the door to the universe will open again, and we'll cross through."

She glanced up, shuddering. A frosty cloud like the contrail from a plane had already begun to form a circle.

He kissed her cheek. "We'll be together for eternity."

CHAPTER TWENTY-FOUR

ABRUPTLY THE STILLNESS became alive with the pounding beat of rap music. Tires squealed and the white glare from headlights whipped across Vanessa's face. Jimena's car plowed across the grass, hurling clumps of mud, then bumped onto the Quad and screeched to a stop. Smoke was still rising from the tire marks on the concrete as Serena and Tianna jumped from the car and faced Hector. Catty slid out, joining them.

Jimena turned off the ignition, and the night fell silent again. She slowly walked around the front of the car and stood with the others.

Vanessa struggled against Hector's arms, trying to pull free and join her friends.

"My arms don't hold you." Hector released her. "The shackles do."

Defeated, Vanessa raised her arms. The thick gold caught the night-lights shining inside Royce Hall and shot reflections into the shadows.

"You're too late!" she yelled to the other Daughters. "I'm bound to him already."

"We're never too late!" Tianna shouted back, squinting, her concentration severe.

Vanessa could feel the bands on her wrists vibrating, then with a sudden flash, they split apart, breaking into chunks and rattling to the ground as sparks cascaded over them.

Tianna folded her arms across her chest. "Nothing holds you now."

Vanessa glanced up. The ring around the moon was no more than a hazy mist, drifting across the sky. She looked at Hector. He did nothing to restrain her. She took a tentative step into the moonlight. When the gentle radiance didn't burn her, she ran to her friends.

"We'd better get ready," Jimena said.

Vanessa turned. Hector was walking toward them, his eyes again dancing with a hellish internal fire. Red-and-orange flames trailed behind him, leaving a sooty path as they swept across the Quad, igniting the grass. Sulfurous smoke trickled into the air.

"What's it like when a demon attacks?" Tianna asked, her focus never leaving Hector.

"We'll find out soon enough," Serena answered, stepping backward.

"How did you find me?" Vanessa asked as she joined arms with Catty and Serena.

"Michael told us you were in trouble." Catty hooked elbows with Tianna.

"Michael?" Vanessa asked.

"That's what I said." Jimena locked arms with Serena. "Since when does Michael know anything that's going on?"

"He doesn't," Vanessa said, realizing Stanton

hadn't abandoned her after all. He had been the shadowy presence inside the hotel. He must have followed her, then sent his Regulator disguised as Michael to find the other Daughters and tell them Vanessa needed help.

"What's with him?" Serena asked, nodding toward Hector. "Why doesn't he attack?"

"Yeah," Catty agreed. "He's creeping me out with those eyes."

Hector continued forward, face determined and grim.

"I don't think we should wait for him to attack first," Vanessa said, remembering the suffocating pressure Hector had bound around her outside the Dungeon.

"I agree," Serena added. "He doesn't look like he's going to fight us the normal way. He's not a Follower, after all."

Vanessa could feel the power throbbing inside her and building. Her nerves and muscles vibrated with its intensity.

They leaned against each other, their energies combining. Then their force shot across the dark like a thunderbolt. It hit Hector and exploded, rocking the ground. Vanessa fell as the heat from the fireball swept over her, the night gleaming with an orange glow from the explosion.

Jimena, Serena, Tianna, and Catty lay sprawled beside her.

"I can't believe we got him so easily." Jimena sat up, studying the black smoke towering into the sky.

"Maybe it's easier to take down a demon." Tianna stood and brushed off her jeans.

"But Maggie said he was perfect." Catty wiped at the soot covering her face.

"I don't know," Vanessa said. "I can still feel his presence."

"Look," Serena whispered, her voice filled with dread and wonder.

Hector stepped through the curtain of flames, small fires dripping from his body. He looked unharmed. No burns on his face or clothes. His brutal expression sent a chill through Vanessa.

"He's too close," Catty warned. "If we try to

do anything now we'll feel a backlash from our power."

"Run," Jimena ordered. "We need to reorganize."

They fled, their feet pounding over grass and down walkways. When they reached Circle Drive near the outskirts of the campus, they slowed, then stopped.

Vanessa bent over, her hands resting on her knees, and tried to catch her breath.

"He's coming," Serena said.

Catty turned to see. "He can't be here already."

Hector advanced at a slow easy pace, his flaming eyes filled with the same cruel promise of death.

Vanessa wrapped her arms through Serena's. "On the count of ten," she said. "Hold your energy back until it's built up."

She could feel the others nodding in agreement. They waited, watching Hector come toward them.

"Now!" Jimena yelled.

The air split with a jolt, shattering the night and turning it as bright as day. The massive discharge speared Hector in the chest. He stumbled backward, then caught himself and continued forward, walking through showering embers, burning leaves, and twigs.

"He absorbed the energy we sent him this time," Vanessa said, astonished. "We made him stronger with our last hit."

Serena stepped next to Vanessa. "We're not supposed to attack first, only defend. Maybe that's what's wrong."

"You want to wait until this one attacks?" Jimena snapped. "He's not a Follower, he's *el diablo*."

"He can't do anything against my power," Tianna assured them. "See that parking structure over there?"

"You think you can knock it down?" Vanessa peered at the huge stacks of concrete slabs, now empty of cars. Electronic eyes scanned the garage entrance. She wondered briefly what security would think when they saw the tapes.

"No," Tianna said, "I'm not that strong, but if I concentrate I bet I can make a pillar or two fall on top of him."

Already Vanessa could feel the ground trembling beneath her feet. The structure swayed. Lights inside flickered on and off. With an ear-splitting crack, the side of a support column collapsed, exposing the steel rods underneath, and an avalanche of concrete and debris rolled over Hector.

Fine sand billowed from the destruction, surging toward them. They stepped back, coughing, their faces covered with dust.

Tianna slapped her hands together as if she had completed a job well done, but her eyes looked exhausted and bloodshot from straining.

"How are we going to explain this?" Jimena was still on probation and Vanessa knew that was troubling her. "Something like this could get me sent back to camp."

"If we're caught, I don't think you'll go alone." Serena seemed concerned. "Look at what we've done."

"Don't worry about it," Tianna said. "The parking structure is still solid. All I have to do is fix the column before we go."

Vanessa watched the mound of rubble. "I don't see any movement."

"Do you think we got him?" Catty asked as they stepped closer.

"Wait," Serena cautioned.

A chunk of concrete tottered, then clattered down the pile. It settled at their feet, rocking back and forth.

They stared at the wreckage in disbelief as large and small pieces rolled away from the top, crashing around them.

"Impossible," Jimena breathed.

Then two grimy hands reached through the rubble. Hector's head poked out, his arms strained, tugging his lower body free. He pulled himself from the wreckage, then turned until he saw them. He kicked the remaining fragments aside and started walking forward, flames seething from beneath his feet.

"Jeez, I think he's mad now," Tianna

muttered. "Maybe I can lose him in the other realm."

"Try it," Vanessa urged her.

Tianna had another ability. Using her telekinetic powers she could lift the veil that divided this world from the next. She struggled to maintain her focus. Vanessa worried about whether or nor Tianna had enough strength left to break down the barrier between the two worlds.

Then everything began to wave like flags on a windy day.

Hector paused as the night buckled and bent. Dried leaves and papers swirled around him, disturbed by the energy Tianna was creating.

Trees, streetlights, and buildings looked as if they were melting. The world shattered around them and they were no longer in Los Angeles but in that other place of churning gray vapors and nothingness.

Vanessa began to shiver. It was colder than she remembered.

But Hector didn't seem to notice that he was no longer on the UCLA campus. He trudged forward, the mists twirling around his feet.

"Hold my hands," Tianna ordered. "We're going back before he figures out what's happening."

Vanessa grabbed hold and steadied herself. Suddenly, they were back in reality, near the demolished parking structure.

"Let's go home." Serena sighed in relief.

"First we'll get Elena and Leda," Vanessa said. "I know where they are."

"Wait," Jimena ordered. "What about the parking structure?"

Within ten minutes, Tianna had it back together. She stretched out on the sidewalk, exhausted, and caught her breath.

The sudden sound of thumping helicopter blades made them alert. The treetops bent as the helicopter passed overhead and directed a white column of light at the parking structure, apparently looking for damage.

"We'd better get out of here," Vanessa warned.

They started running, darting from shadow to shadow, and continued until they turned the corner and saw Jimena's car parked illegally where she had left it. A campus police car was pulled alongside, two officers walking toward it.

Jimena signaled for the others to hide behind a line of bushes. Vanessa knelt near an oleander, its fuchsia flowers bobbing in front of her.

Then the night turned tomb quiet, the atmosphere becoming thick and heavy. Vanessa knew the others were feeling it, too.

She glanced at the campus police.

The large bulky one's hand rested over the butt of his gun, his eyes vigilant and searching for the danger.

"What is it?" Catty asked.

The night shimmered as Hector stepped through a rip in reality near Jimena's car. He paused, head turning, looking for them, then he spied Vanessa and continued forward, the expression on his face unreadable.

The officers charged him, guns drawn,

ordering him to stop. But when they saw the flames in his eyes they hesitated, stunned, then ran back to their car, dove in, and sped away before they had even closed their doors.

"Any ideas?" Jimena asked.

"Yeah," Catty yelled. "Run!"

"It's no use," Serena said, grabbing Catty's arm. "Look at our amulets. They're not even glowing. Nothing we do against him works."

"We need to at least get away from here," Vanessa said. "I'll make us invisible."

"Hurry!" Catty said.

Vanessa could feel their hands tightening on her as she focused her thoughts on becoming invisible. Her molecules pulsed, trying to pull free from gravity, but now she had four people to take with her. She concentrated until her vision went gray from the effort; then, blinking, she looked down. Her hands were starting to fade.

Catty's arms quivered as Vanessa's power flowed into her cells, then her body appeared to evaporate.

Soon all of them were no more than dust

flitting in the air. They floated upward, a delicate mist curling into the night sky.

Vanessa led them away, happiness surging through her.

But as she rocketed over Powell Library, she felt a pressure wrap around her as if a net had entrapped her, the mesh tightening, forcing her molecules to gather. She sensed the others struggling against it, too, as they dove toward the ground. If they materialized at this height, the fall would kill them.

CHAPTER TWENTY-FIVE

VANESSA SPED DOWN. She was still four feet in the air, the others gliding behind her, when the air crushed around her, ramming her molecules together painfully. She fell to the sidewalk, skidding into the grass, her breath knocked from her. Serena fell on top of her and rolled beside her. Catty smashed to the ground a few inches away. Jimena hit the concrete with a loud thwack and moaned.

Tianna was the only one who managed to stay on her feet, running to a stop. She walked back to them, her shadow blocking the glare from the streetlight. She placed her hands on her hips. "We didn't get far enough away."

Hector's steps echoed in the distance.

Vanessa closed her eyes, resting her cheek in the dew-wet grass, her nostrils filling with the scent of damp earth.

Catty licked at the trickle of blood running from her lip.

"Sorry," Vanessa whispered.

Catty tried to smile. "I've done worse to you in my landings when we time traveled."

"What happens when he gets us?" Serena asked, sitting up.

"He won't." Vanessa rubbed at the pain in the back of her neck.

Hector turned the corner. Smoke wreathed his body and slipped into the night in a thin veil that curled around them. The sulfurous smell was nauseating, and now it had a cloyingly sweet aroma mixed with it.

Vanessa's eyes watered.

Jimena stood and grabbed Serena's arm, pulling her to her feet. A bruise spread over the side of her face. For the first time Vanessa saw an inkling of fear cross her eyes.

"We have to do something," Catty said, waving away the smoke.

"But what?" Tianna asked. "Nothing we've tried has worked so far."

"Maybe if I could stop Vanessa before she picks up the flame," Catty suggested. "That might change everything."

"I told you about your visit from the future," Vanessa said. "You were sucked back into the tunnel before you could warn me."

But already Catty's eyes were dilating as if a powerful force surged inside her. "This time I'll know what to expect."

The minute hand on her watch began moving backward as a black line appeared in the air above her. It opened, sucking Catty inside, and closed with a flash of bluish-white light and the crackle of thunder.

"What happened to Hector?" Serena asked.

Vanessa turned back. He was gone. "Do you think he went after Catty to bring her back?"

"I don't think he decided to quit chasing us just like that," Tianna said, her face gaunt and worn. "If he can get out of that other realm, then chances are he can open the tunnel."

Vanessa felt the hairs on the back of her neck rise. "Catty's coming back already."

The hollow gap opened in the air in front of them and Catty tumbled from the black emptiness inside, falling in a heap on the walkway. She glanced up at Vanessa, terror on her face. She looked exactly as Vanessa remembered her from that night in her room.

"Any luck?" Serena asked, but her face didn't look hopeful.

"I got back," Catty explained. "I landed in Vanessa's backyard, opened her back door, and ran up to her bedroom, but she wasn't home. Then I saw her through her bedroom window and tapped on the glass, trying to get her attention, but already I could feel something dragging me back." She looked at Vanessa. "It was just like you said. I struggled to stay and warn you, but his power was too strong to resist."

Jimena let out a whistle.

Vanessa turned sharply as Hector reappeared.

He paused. She had an uncanny feeling that he was savoring the moment before he destroyed them.

Then she felt that suffocating pressure tightening around her.

"It feels like I'm breathing molasses." Tianna wheezed, her chest heaving as if she were struggling to pull in air.

The pressure continued to build.

"He's suffocating us." Serena choked out.

Vanessa looked at her friends. If it weren't for her, they wouldn't be in danger. A chill passed through her as the solution presented itself. She pushed through the heavy air back to Hector.

He waited for her as if this had always been his plan.

When she stood next to him, she spoke. "I'll go with you, but let my friends live."

Immediately, the oppressive air was gone.

CHAPTER TWENTY-SIX

"VANESSA, DON'T GO with him!" Catty ran after her, but stopped abruptly as if she had slammed into an invisible wall. Her hands pressed against the air, like a mime trapped in a box. Within seconds the others were with her, shoving against the transparent barricade, their voices muffled as they screamed for Vanessa to come back to them. Tianna tried to use her telekinetic powers to bring down the barrier, but the force field remained.

"Thank you, Vanessa," Hector said, his eyes

looking human again. "I've lived for centuries without companionship."

Vanessa could almost pity him. She wondered how it would feel to be alone, casting about the planets and stars, traveling endlessly in the vast void of space. Then with a jolt she realized that within minutes she would know. Hot tears slid down her cheeks. Her legs began trembling.

"Don't cry. You'll learn to love me, I promise." His voice sounded sincere and comforting. "I haven't forgotten how to love."

He glanced up and she followed his gaze. A frosty line was circling the moon.

Vanessa stared at the stars, once beautiful, now seeming desolate and far away. "I don't want to go," she said softly. "If you love me, can't you leave and let me stay?"

"I can't be without you," he whispered. "I have loved you since that first night when I stole into your house to see who the Atrox had sent me to destroy."

"You woke me up?" Vanessa remembered the sensation of someone nudging her awake.

"Yes, and I put the fingerprints on the glass to scare you, hoping I would find you as brave as you were beautiful. You didn't disappoint me."

"But I ran," she said, hoping she could prove that she wasn't worthy of him. "I wasn't brave."

"You only ran after you had become invisible and I tried to mix my molecules with yours. It was a new experience for you, and even the bravest warrior is wise to retreat when she encounters the unexpected."

Vanessa sighed.

Hector continued. "Melding with you was a luxurious feeling I can never forget. After that night, I had to have you. So I went to the Atrox with another plan and asked to have you as my reward if I succeeded."

"What other plan?" Vanessa asked.

"As soon as the circle is complete, you and I will meld together, but before we leave earth, we'll destroy the other Daughters."

"No!" Vanessa cried, remembering the crushing pressure Hector had wrapped around her

earlier that night. The Daughters would be pow-
erless against him—against the two of them.

"It will be our first act as one entity," he
assured her. "The Atrox will be pleased."

She struggled, trying to pull free. "Run!
Go!" she shouted, trying to warn her friends,
but they apparently couldn't hear her.

Hector pointed up.

She didn't need to look up to know the circle was almost complete. Her molecules pinched
together, repulsed by the nearness of Hector's
loosening cells.

His molecules became restless, pulling out.
The power of his transformation flowed
through her in waves as he began to dissolve.
Her heartbeat quickened and her lungs filled
with his strange, sweet, sulfurous smell, at once
enticing and repugnant.

Against her will, her fingers and feet began
to fade, aroused by the vigorous change in
Hector's body. His hands now had the grainy
quality of old newsprint photos. He cupped her
cheeks tenderly, his skin prickling against her.

"Wait," she whimpered. "Give me one last look at earth and let me tell my friends good-bye."

His eyes, still intact, glanced at her with understanding. He let their molecules pull together, two complete and separate forms, then he brushed his hand through her hair.

"Say your farewells," he whispered. The look in his eyes made her think he actually felt sorry for what he was doing to her. Could he really love her?

She wanted to appear brave as she mouthed her good-byes, so she stuck her hands in her pockets to hide their trembling. As she did, her fingers sank into a fine powder. Then she remembered the ash she had taken from Maggie's fire. She felt a trickle of hope. It might act like holy water. It could purify Hector, especially now that he was no longer wearing the shackles.

"Take a deep breath," he said. "The circle is complete."

She nodded and gathered the ash into her hands.

His molecules percolated against her as if sharp needles were bombarding her, urging her to change.

She concentrated. She needed to stay whole for her plan to work, but her feet and legs swirled dangerously. She waited until his face became a spectral form, then she threw the first fistful of ash at him, the fine particles merging with his cells.

A horrified look crossed his phantom face. His mouth stretched, and a scream skated from his throat, high-pitched and painful to her ears. Then he slammed back together, his hands digging into his cheeks.

He stopped abruptly, stunned, and looked at her with an expression of sadness and regret. Then his eyelids fluttered and she imagined that she was seeing the person he had once been, a brave and kindhearted soldier. She felt his gratitude before he closed his eyes.

When he opened them again, the blaze burning inside him gave off a divine light, as if the evil had been pushed aside. Tendrils of smoke curled around his face, but without the stench of sulfur or decay. Orange flames tinged with blue and white licked from his mouth, nose, and ears.

Finally, an inferno engulfed him.

The barrier fell and Catty ran to her. "What did you do?"

"I released him." Vanessa opened her fist and showed Catty the gray-white ash. "Maggie had used this to purify me. It must have done the same to Hector."

Jimena, Serena, and Tianna gathered around his pyre.

Glittering white flames continued to consume his body until there was only smoke and ash.

"What should we do with his ashes?" Serena asked.

"Take them," Vanessa answered. "I know someone who will want them."

"You do?" Catty asked.

The others looked at her oddly.

"Hector was Maggie's lover once," she said softly. Then she told them the story.

By the time Jimena parked in the alley behind the Corona Hotel, Vanessa had finished telling them everything about Maggie and Hector. They found Elena and Leda tied in an upstairs room, and after they had taken them home, they carried Hector's ashes to Maggie. She asked them to leave so she could be alone to mourn.

Outside Maggie's apartment, Vanessa looked up at the moon. "Let's start celebrating," she announced, feeling happier than she had in weeks.

The others turned and looked at her.

"Celebrate what?" Catty asked.

"My birthday." Vanessa grinned.

"I can't." Catty looked at her wristwatch. "It's too late."

"Yeah, it's almost morning," Jimena added. "I gotta get some sleep."

"Aren't you tired?" Serena asked.

"Forget it," Vanessa answered and fell back in the air, letting her molecules fade until she was only a silky vapor streaming into the night. She cruised toward Melrose Avenue. The street was empty now except for a few homeless punkers, their thick boots breaking the silence of the night.

She continued on, reluctant to go home to an empty house, but when she arrived, the porch light blazed a welcome. She pulled her molecules together and drifted down to the yard, then hurried to the back door and stepped inside.

"Mom?" Vanessa called as she walked into the warm kitchen, the smell of coffee greeting her.

Her mother stood over the sink, staring out the window. She turned abruptly. "Vanessa!" Her eyes were red, her hair looked tousled as if she had been raking worried hands through it.

"Is everything okay?" Vanessa asked, wondering what bad thing had happened now.

Her mother rushed to her, her cold hands touching Vanessa's arms, and then she held her tightly. "I was so worried about you."

"I'm sorry," Vanessa said.

"It wasn't just that." Her mother sat in the chair in front of her worktable.

"What happened?" Vanessa asked.

"I was at work when suddenly I had this awful feeling that I was never going to see you again." Her mother stopped abruptly. "For goodness sake, Vanessa, what did you do to yourself? You're covered with dust and soot."

"Don't you remember that Catty and I were camping in her backyard tonight?" Vanessa lied.

"What's this on your arms?" Her mother's voice seemed nearly panicked now.

Vanessa glanced down. Red sores circled her wrists where the bands had been bound to her, and blisters gathered on the ring finger of her left hand, but the demon's mark was completely gone.

"They're just burns, Mom," Vanessa said, embellishing her lie. "We were making S'mores on a Bunsen burner, and I did this. The pain was bad so I decided to come home."

Her mother pulled her over to the sink, found a pack of bandages and turned on the water. "All the way around your wrists? If you were trying to do some of those new scar tattoos, I'll send you to private school so fast—this is

Catty's mother's fault. She never bothers to supervise the two of you."

Vanessa stopped listening. Things felt normal again. On impulse she hugged her mother.

Her mother stopped complaining and smiled.

Then Vanessa pulled back and looked at the outfit she was wearing. "Mom, those pink leggings over black tights and that gray felt skirt—"

"I know," her mother interrupted. "It's not going to work. Hit or miss. I can't have successes all the time, but you don't know which looks will be the new style unless you try them. Which reminds me. Have you seen a blue dress with a low back and slits up the side? I can't find it, and I have someone who wants to buy it."

Vanessa shook her head. "Maybe you can sew another one. It was a winner."

Her mother smiled and glanced down at her watch. "Let's call it a day. It's almost time for the sun to rise."

Vanessa nodded and went upstairs. She showered, surprised to find the floral design still tattooed over her heart. She sat on her window seat, combing her hair as she watched the moon set. Tomorrow she turned sixteen. They had stopped Hector, but she wondered if another demon would ever come for her and release the spirit of Pandora that lived inside her.

CHAPTER TWENTY-SEVEN

VANESSA AWOKE, THREW BACK her covers, and swung her legs over the edge of her bed in one easy motion. Late-afternoon sunshine fell peacefully through the slats in her shutters. She glanced at her clock radio. A white envelope sat in front of the readout with her name across the front.

She ripped it open. It was a birthday card from her mother. Her birthday! She looked at the clock again. It read four o'clock. She couldn't believe she had almost slept the day away.

Then she studied the picture of Michael on her dresser. He had promised they would spend her birthday together.

She jumped from bed, yanked on the jeans, T-shirt, and blazer she had been saving for this day, then wrapped her hair on top of her head and spiked the ends. She rushed downstairs.

A huge birthday cake sat in the middle of the kitchen table. She ran her finger along the bottom and stuck the creamy frosting into her mouth. Sweet vanilla flavors awakened her taste buds.

Then her eyes caught a note from her mother. Michael had called three times!

She grabbed her shades and keys, found her shoes, and ran out the door. Her lips moved, practicing what she would say as she walked over to Michael's house. Anyone looking at her would think she was talking to herself, but she didn't care. She had only one thing on her mind and it had to happen today.

The scent of honeysuckle greeted her as she stepped on Michael's porch and knocked on the door. She stopped abruptly, holding her fist in midair, and grimaced. She hadn't knocked; she had pounded like the big bad wolf demanding entrance.

The door swung open. Michael glanced at her, a look of surprise on his darkly tanned face. He had cut his hair, and she liked the spiky look.

"Vanessa," he spoke her name as if he was happy to see her, then his arms opened and he hugged her. "I'm sorry I didn't get to call you to say good-bye before I left. There was a mix-up on the times, and I barely made the bus."

She squeezed against him. "You don't know how much I've missed you," she said, delighting in the warmth of his body.

"I've missed you, too." He took her hand and pulled her inside. "Happy Birthday."

He kissed her gently. She closed her eyes, enjoying the feel of his lips on hers, then her eyes popped open, and she yanked away from him.

"What?" he asked, his eyes dreamy.

"Where did we first meet?" she asked. She needed to know that this was the real Michael.

"Spanish class. Why?"

"Just checking." She leaned forward and kissed him again. Her molecules buzzed with pleasure, and she wondered if he could feel the vibration. She breathed in his clean soap smell and found the courage to tell him what she wanted for her birthday.

"Michael, there's something special I want for my birthday."

He nodded. "What?"

Her molecules started to float in slow easy circles. She knew if she looked down her feet would be a dusty swarm. "I've been trying to tell you all week."

"All week?" He looked at her oddly. "I was gone."

"Right." She recovered. "I mean I've been practicing what I wanted to say to you for weeks now."

"You've known that long and didn't tell me?" He looked baffled.

She nodded and tried to find the words to tell him now. "I want . . . I want us to have more in our relationship."

Now he was quiet, staring at her with that look that made her want to forget what she was saying and just kiss him. He smoothed his hands up her sides. "What do you mean?" he asked quietly.

"I . . ." she started and stopped. The molecules in her feet were totally out of control now, and she could feel the prickle traveling up her legs. She stomped her foot, trying to force them back in order.

Michael looked at her oddly. "Is your foot okay?"

She caught his face between her hands before he could look down. She took a deep breath. She was never, ever going to be able to say the words.

"Look, my mom's going to be out on a night shoot," she said. "Why don't we go over to my house, and I'll just show you."

He looked at her for a long time, and she thought he was going to tell her no.

"Please, Michael." She tried to keep her voice steady. Was he going to make her beg? She had thought he liked her more than that.

Then he smiled. "Let me get my car keys."

She leaned back against the door jamb, breathing through her pursed lips, and tried to calm her racing heart as his footsteps pounded up the stairs. She wondered if she would have enough nerve once they were back at her house.

New panic overtook her as she heard him coming back down the stairs, jingling his keys. She hadn't thought this through. Should she just do it as soon as they were in the house, or fix something to eat first? Maybe they should watch TV. She didn't know.

"Help me," she whispered to no one in particular, suddenly realizing she was in over her head.

Michael joined her and wrapped his arm around her waist. "What are you waiting for? Come on."

He pulled her outside, shut the front door, then hurried her to the old Volkswagen bus painted with psychedelic pink and orange flowers. He helped her into the passenger's side but before closing the door, he gave her a slow lazy smile. "You sure, Vanessa?"

She swallowed, certain he had heard the click in her throat, then nodded. "I'm sure."

He hesitated. "I really l—like you, Vanessa."

His expression told her that he had almost used a more powerful word; the one she hoped to hear someday. He leaned in and kissed her cheek, his lips lingering before he pulled back and slammed the door.

She settled into the seat, trying to steady her breathing. Her stomach felt as if she were going over a free fall on a roller coaster. She turned as the driver's-side door opened and Michael crawled in. The thought of being alone with him made her heart skip a beat. She tensed, trying to decide what she would do when they got to her house.

"Ready?" he asked as the engine came to life.

She nodded and the car pulled away from the curb.

* * *

Ten minutes later, they stood on the porch at her front door. She was glad now that she hadn't left the porch light on. Darkness hid them.

He leaned down, lips teasing, hovering inches from hers, and then he kissed her. A sweet ache rushed through her.

"Let's go inside," he whispered.

She nodded and pulled away, digging her keys from her pocket. She unlocked the front door and they slipped inside.

As she reached to flick on the light switch, Michael caught her hand and stopped her. He used his foot to shut the door, then tenderly pressed her against the wall and kissed her again, his tongue darting over her lips, his body warm against hers.

A sudden flash of light made Vanessa's eyes pop open. The noise was overwhelming.

"What the—" Michael exclaimed and jerked away from her.

Vanessa pushed in front of him, ready to protect him from the danger, but what she saw made no sense to her.

CHAPTER TWENTY-EIGHT

CATTY, TIANNA, JIMENA, and Serena threw confetti and streamers. The living room was filled with pink and purple balloons. Confusion rushed through Vanessa as she saw faces of kids from her Geometry class and soccer team.

Everyone was shouting at once and then she finally understood what they were yelling.

"Surprise!"

Collin and Derek pushed a cart from the kitchen. A birthday cake with sixteen lit candles sat on top. They nearly knocked over a stack of presents as they rolled it to her.

Her mother shoved through the crowd. "Happy birthday, Vanessa." She beamed. "Did you really think we'd forgotten?"

Vanessa swallowed hard and tried to keep the blush from rising to her cheeks. She glanced at Michael. He looked as dazed as she felt, his face red under his deep tan.

Catty rushed over to her and squeezed her tightly. "So now you know what we were talking about."

"Yeah," Tianna said. "You got so upset when you thought we were talking about you."

"You never suspected we were planning a party for you?" Jimena asked. "*¿De veras?*"

"Never," Vanessa answered, feeling over-whelmed with joy.

Catty playfully punched her. "It was so hard lying to my best friend, and every time Tianna and I had to sneak off to order your cake or birthday balloons or write out invitations, you always wanted to tag along."

"We had to make up lies." Tianna laughed. "We weren't very good about it, and you kept giving us the evil eye like you knew. Catty almost told you. She was miserable because she thought her best friend was upset with her."

"Happy birthday!" Catty hugged her and gave Vanessa a box decorated with the moon and stars. BEST FRIENDS FOREVER was drawn on the lid.

"We didn't even tell Michael," Serena added.

"You should have," Michael said, rubbing his forehead.

"No way," Jimena said. "You would have told Vanessa."

"But how did you know I'd be here?" Vanessa asked.

"We didn't. We just figured you'd be doing homework," Serena said and handed her a present.

"Like always," Catty teased. "Then we got here, and your mom didn't know where you were. She was going to get you out of the house by taking you down to Baskin-Robbins to pick up ice cream for your cake."

Vanessa unwrapped Serena's present and pulled out the pink-and-black bowling shirt she had seen Serena show the others outside Aardvark's Odd Ark on Melrose Avenue. "Thanks," she said with a laugh. "I love it."

The party was wonderful, but Vanessa still had one thing she needed to do before the day was over. She pulled Michael into the kitchen and took a deep breath. "Okay, I'm going to tell you what I want for my birthday—just please don't laugh. I've been trying to say it for so long now."

"Tell me." He caressed her cheek.

"I want to sing." There it was, out in the open.

"You?" He looked dumbfounded.

"I asked you not to laugh." She couldn't breathe. If he made fun of her now, she'd vanish and probably never become visible again.

"I'm not laughing, but you surprised me," he said. "You never showed any interest in singing before."

"I want you to hear me now." She watched him carefully.

He nodded. "All right."

"It's a song I wrote myself," she whispered, the words barely coming from her throat.

He looked impressed. "You wrote a song?"

"If it's good enough I want you to let me sing with your band." She had finally said what she had been trying to tell him for weeks. Her heart beat like mad as she waited for his answer.

CHAPTER TWENTY-NINE

F RIDAY NIGHT, VANESSA walked past the line of kids waiting to go inside Planet Bang. She was with the band tonight and didn't have to pay to enter. She followed Michael through a side door. They walked down a dark hallway, and then they stood in the crowded dance area.

Lasers broke across the smoky mist in red, blue, and orange spikes, repeating the beat of the music. She tugged at her leather choker, but she couldn't seem to breathe properly. She glanced at Michael. He had seemed so sure when he told her she was great; her songs a blend of rock and soul. Tonight she was adding punk to the mix. Now she felt panicked as they walked toward the stage.

She kept casting sideways glances at the kids checking her out as she climbed onto the platform at the side of the dance floor. She no longer looked like the ultimate beach girl. Her gorgeous surfer blond hair was texturized and strewn with pink and purple dreadlocks, her arms heavy with bangles. Would her friends accept this new Vanessa?

She had spent the afternoon, trying on clothes, casting one thing aside and taking up another before settling on hip-hugging jeans and a skimpy halter top that showed off her flat stomach and the floral tattoo on her chest. A bindi circled her belly button, and Catty had painted tattoos on her arms. She looked tough, and she liked the look, but it wasn't about trying to entice the guys. There was more to life than that, and she hoped girls would hear it in her lyrics.

Michael took her hand. "You said you

wanted to shock everyone." He smiled. "I guess you've broken out of your mold tonight."

She nodded and tried not to look at the surprised faces or the pointing fingers. Even her mother was here, standing in the back with her friends from the movie set.

Serena, Jimena, Tianna, and Catty gathered at the edge of the stage.

"Scope it out," Jimena yelled. "We got some real talent here tonight."

"Knock 'em dead," Serena added, grinning.

Michael handed her the microphone, then kissed her cheek. "Sing for them the way you sang for me."

She nodded.

He clasped her hand. "Just go for it and don't worry about anything."

She bit her lip and wished her mouth didn't feel so dry "I can't believe I'm so nervous." She took a deep breath.

"It's not nerves," Michael answered. "It's anticipation. You're going to let your soul speak tonight and that creeping feeling in your stomach is your soul crawling up to take over your brain. Let it rip."

Then the music stopped and the deejay hopped onto the stage. "Let's give it up for our new singer, Vanessa Cleveland."

Everyone yelled, whooped, and stomped. Vanessa turned back to Michael, surprised he hadn't even had the deejay introduce himself or his band.

"It's your night," he mouthed back at her and then his fingers were on his bass guitar, running up and down the frets. The vapors caught the light show. Blue and red stabbed the air in time to the punk-rock beat.

Vanessa turned to the crowd and lifted the microphone. If she was ever going to do it, she had to do it now. She could no longer live her life as the Vanessa Cleveland she had been, always cautious, always doing what was right, sensible, and expected. She had to let her other side out.

The first song was intense and rousing, the beat fast. She opened her mouth, terrified no sound would come, but then she let out one electrifying wail and began the first line. She could feel the barrier fall between her and the audience. Magic was working as she continued to sing about a heart filled with resentment and hot jealousy. She could feel their emotions swelling in the room.

She glanced down at Tianna and saw a wry smile on her face, as if she understood the song was about her.

The lyrics poured from Vanessa, and she felt supercharged. She continued singing and it was as if she had let the deepest part of herself fly. It was true what Hector had told her; she was born to spread sorrow, but not in the way he might have imagined. She could make people feel their sadness through her music, but she also gave them hope, dreams, and desires.

When she opened her eyes again, she glanced at her friends gathered nearby and knew they were feeling the part of her that belonged to Pandora.

Her voice rose. This was what she had been longing for. Here was the passion she needed to express.

The song ended. The entire crowd was whistling and cheering wildly.

Michael nudged her and whispered into her ear. "You're a rock goddess."

She smiled. "If you only knew."

Don't miss the next

DAUGHTERS OF THE MOON book,

Possession

SERENA STARED INTO Stanton's blue eyes, breathing in the familiar scent of him. She took a quick step back, not understanding her chaotic emotions or her disturbing physical attraction to him. She was a Daughter of the Moon, and it was her mission to protect people from Followers like Stanton.

His hand reached up to touch her cheek, but she batted it away before he could.

"You summoned me, Serena, and now you're backing away," he said, his eyes looking at her with the gentleness she remembered.

"I didn't call you," she answered, feeling miserable and happy at the same time.

"She needs your help," Jimena interrupted.

"Serena," he repeated her name longingly.

"No, I don't." Serena spoke with more anger than she had intended. She could feel the icy spirit of the Atrox surging through Stanton. His evil pulsed in the air. Couldn't the others sense it? She hated him for what he had become, but other familiar emotions were surfacing, and she didn't want him to see her pain.

"I'm sorry," he said softly.

Her head jerked back, studying him. Had he caught her sadness before she had even been able to hide it? Maybe it was impossible to conceal anything from him now.

Her moon amulet cast a ghostly light across his face, but it didn't seem to bother him. He cocked an eyebrow and tried to ease into her mind as he had done so many times before, but she stopped him and refused to listen to his apology.

"I can't trust you now," she said. "You betrayed me."

A flicker of hurt crossed his eyes, but she knew that had to be an illusion. A person without a soul couldn't feel such emotion.

"You have the power to look in my mind," he said. "If you do, you'll know."

She watched him, not sure what she should do.

"I'm waiting." He stepped closer, his mind completely open to her.

She could feel the heat radiating off his body and took a deep breath, ignoring her aching need to embrace him. He had freely chosen to return to the Atrox. He was her enemy now.

"I haven't done anything to make you distrust me," he said.

Serena's breath caught. Did Stanton still love her? How could he? She couldn't believe him anymore.

"I'm telling you the truth," he insisted, as if he had read her doubts.

Serena gazed into his eyes and steadied her voice. "Next time, we meet as enemies."

He stared at her, eyes desperately sad. "The only person I love is now my fiercest enemy."

She forced herself to nod and turn away from him.

He leaned back, blending with the darkness, and became a black mist, hissing into the air.

She blinked, trying not to think of him, but she couldn't forget the defeated look on his face.

LYNNE EWING is a screenwriter who also counsels troubled teens. In addition to writing all of the books in the Daughters of the Moon series, she is the author of two ALA Quick Picks: *Drive-By* and *Party Girl*. Ms. Ewing lives in Los Angeles, California.